I0593620

Hunter's Moon:

Jax's Retribution

by

V.J.Garland

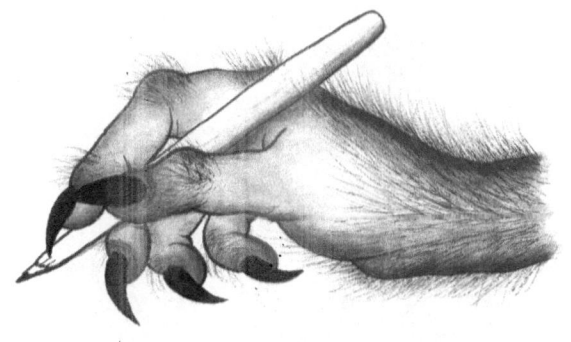

V.J.Garland

Hunter's Moon:

Jax's

Jax' Retribution is a part
of a series.

See Hunter's Moon for the
first instalment of
heartbreak and anarchy.

V.J.GARLAND

Hunter's Moon

Jax' Retribution (Hunter's Moon) Book #2 by V.J.Garland

Published by V.J.Garland

https://vanessajgarland.com/

For permissions contact: vgarland89@outlook.com

Book Cover illustrations by Umar Setiawan

Editor: Tiffany Pelletier

ISBN: 978-0-6487069-6-0

First Edition.

Genre: Thriller/Fantasy/Horror/Romance

Summary: Still reeling from the events on Cannon beach, Jax is faced with a difficult future. The town is left in pieces and it's up to him and a group of old friends to ensure the safety of all who escaped death. But the surviving werewolves have an unexpected advantage... Jax will face the decision of a lifetime bringing him to his knees.

Printed in Australia.

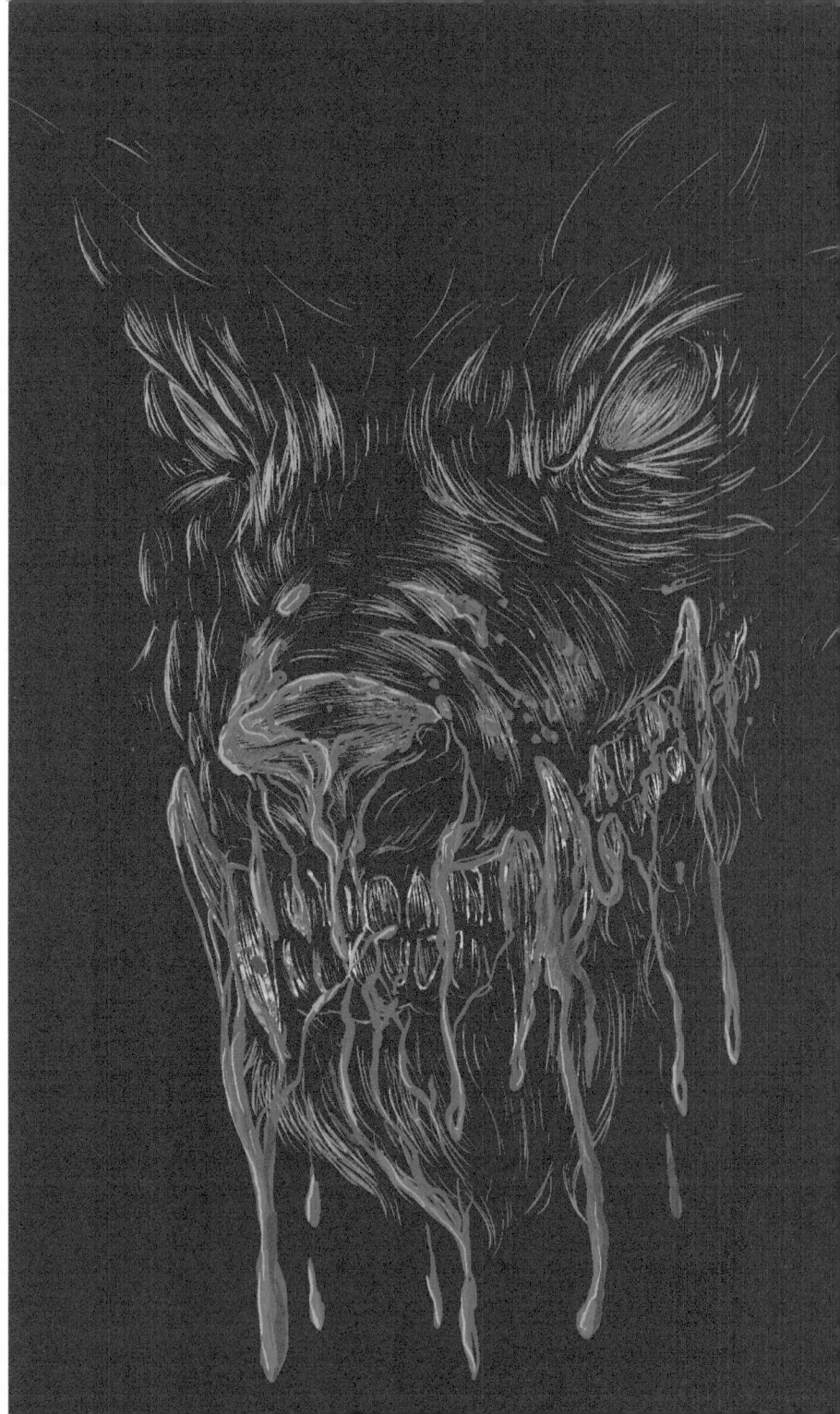

For those who risk it all, at any, and every cost.

For the dreamers who dare to dream to inflict change not for their own gain.

For the person not filming their generosity and walking away with only warmth in their hearts.

V.J.Garland

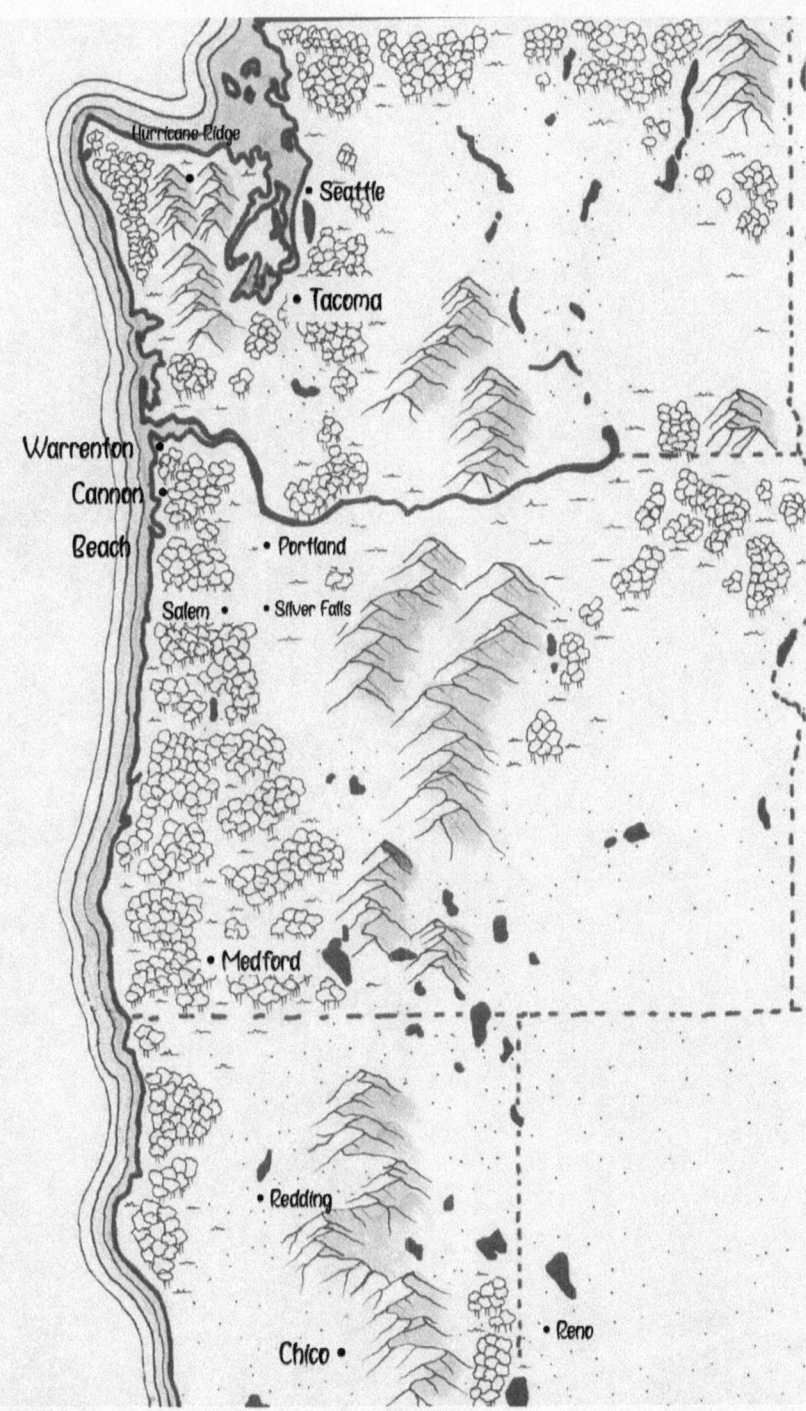

V.J.Garland

CHAPTER ONE

JAX

The puddles of blood were absorbed by the sand quicker than it could flow from their bodies. I felt a burning pain in my gums.

Lupe's body was lifeless, and Noah was slowly becoming nothing but ash that was quickly dragged out to sea by the wind.

Sirens wailed and hotel guests burst onto the beach, alarmed by all the mayhem.

What disturbed me most, were the short seconds of silence after life left every being on this beach. The instant silence was deafening. Even the crashing of the waves seemed to subside, like the shock became a blockage in my ears.

Paramedics rushed toward me, and police with torches and spotlights on their cars tried desperately to conceal the scene. Bystanders were pointing and covering their children's eyes. I recognized the medics bandaging me, they had been to my hospital numerous times and on the very rare occasion we'd have drinks at the local bar with other co-workers.

"Dr. Collins? Are you okay?" Celinde asked.

I was numb, non-verbal, and my leg was deeply gashed, four perfect strikes that were superficially worse than they felt.

'Jax!" Carrie shook me, trying to pull me out of the shock.

"Carrie, let's get him on the gurney," Celinde ordered.

Carrie pulled the gurney closer, and together they assisted me up and into the ambulance.

As I was hauled into the van, police approached, and one jumped inside with us. The spotlights clearly illuminated what had unfolded. There was crimson sand everywhere, and Penny's limbs were strewn over several meters.

I knew these people in the ambulance with me, not well, mostly professionally. Except for Kyle, he was my grade school best friend from Tacoma, who I had convinced to move out here with me.

Inevitably, we had drifted over the years as we both got caught up in college and eventually work.

"Dr. Collins, I need to know what happened here," said Kyle, a sheriff's deputy in our region. He had failed his bar exam and opted for a different take on law.

"She's dead…" I muttered.

I barely felt the words leave my lips. It wasn't until Kyle gripped me by the shoulders that I realized I wasn't whispering, I was screaming. The ride back to Warrenton felt like it went by in a blink. We rolled into the hospital where I had been hours before with Lupe.

But it felt different and, the pang in my mouth worsened. My hands ached and, my eyes were dry and itchy. The lights that lit the Emergency entry were blinking and there was an absence of sound—until there wasn't. I could hear my blood pulsing through my veins and Carrie's heart rate quickened as she entered the oddly quiet hall first.

I was still on the gurney, Celinde pushing from behind with Kyle. Papers and files were flailing under the fans that normally were never running. Clumps of hair were hooked around one fan and it was soaked red with blood.

"Stop here," Kyle ordered as he pulled out his gun.

I climbed down from the gurney and followed behind him. It was becoming increasingly difficult to ignore the cranial pain. My skull felt like it was going to explode any second, my skin felt tighter like I didn't belong in it, and there was a sensation of crawling beneath it that made me itch.

"Jax? Stay here," he ordered.

I ignored him though. I knew what was inside. I didn't know how many, but I was well aware of what was happening to my body.

"No, you should stay with the girls," I said gripping his shoulder and pressing him to the wall.

"Go!" I snarled.

He listened out of fear and backed away slowly.

Fangs had broken through my gums, and I could taste my own blood. I smelt fear in the air that led me to the lunchroom. Huge beasts paced back and forth, and I could hear the shallow breathing of three humans trapped in the freezer.

I had no desire to be this monster. I knew from what Lupe had told me that I could fight it back if I didn't feed. But the smell of blood was mouth-watering. I peered around the corner and the other werewolves caught my scent. They were fully formed and playfully tossing chairs and tables at the freezer door, taunting the humans.

If I wanted to blend in, I had to trust myself. I let out a howl, to signal the others to leave before they were noticed. My hands began to break and remold into muscular, hairy weapons. I heard Carrie and the others race for the ambulance, but one of the wolves had heard them too. It wasn't long till the other two werewolves followed after him.

Unlocking the freezer would be like signing a death warrant as I punch in the control system hoping to shut off the power. The humans should be able to last till morning if that stopped working. I turned and raced outside hoping the ambulance had left safely, but what awaited me was gunfire and a hoard of police vehicles. There were men with shotguns and werewolves pounced from walls to cars, tearing down people faster than police backup could arrive. Guns snapped like twigs in the wolves' murder mittens. My transformation wasn't complete, I wasn't over the edge like them…not yet.

Kyle spotted me in the hallway of the ER entry and dashed towards me—tackling me to the ground.

"What the fuck have you done?" He roared as he stared frightfully, my yellow bloodshot eyes burned under the fluorescent lighting as I gazed up at him.

"You have to lock me up. Now!" I growled as I showed him my hands.

"Fuck," he gasped.

He wrestled handcuffs around my wrists—a tight fit as my form continually grew. He and two other officers got me into a cruiser and raced me away to the sheriff's office, the massacre still unfolding as we sped off down the road.

"Hurry! I can't fight it much longer," I yelled.

It took everything out of me not to evolve—that would be the easy option. The pain would be momentary, and then I'd be free to be careless and unleash.

All the things I didn't want to be.

I wanted to rewind the day and save my little brother.

He didn't need to be caught up in this situation.

He shouldn't have even been home for dinner. He was meant to be at work.

My heart raced harder, faster—I was uncertain if it was due to my imminent transformation or the suffocating feeling I felt when I revisited the image of Lupe impaled beneath the weight of Noah's wolf form.

The ride to the station was bumpy as gunfire continued out the back of the cruiser towards the single lone wolf who continued to chase us.

"Kyle, stop! Let me out," I ordered.

My wrists swelled again, snapping the cuffs as if they were cornflakes under the heel of a boot. My gums tore open, and fangs forced their way through. The other two officers froze as I snarled, then slipped into the front of the car just as the other wolf pounced onto the roof.

I was now too big to get out of a door and so I ripped my claws through the roof as panic and disorder ensued around me.

I leaped through the opening of the roof, cutting my legs further on my way out, only to be met with an unfriendly paw with razor-sharp blades to the face and teeth-gnashing violently towards me, he clumsily bounded upon the bumper of the vehicle slipping off each time unable to maintain his grip.

I leaped down to the ground and in seconds my body had redefined all human masculinity I had hours before, I was taller, wider, my reflexes were faster, nothing was impossible—I felt indestructible.

I was far larger than the other werewolf and he backed away as I towered over him. Every lift of my leg that impounded the ground was like the weight of a small car. The soil jumped around my feet as my claws rattled the dirt.

The other wolf's eyes were orange with thick blood-stained tears drudging down his face. I approached him with force, my claws thick, callused, and ready to carve through him. His snarls were weak and pitiful as he curled his shoulders down, flexing his jaw revealing his fangs.

I stomped forward and with a light swipe, I had flung him into the side of the car, he tore his claws down the side of a door to slow his pace.

He caught the scent of the officers in the car. He tried forcefully to enter through the roof, but I pounced over the car, gripping the fur from his back, and slamming him down onto a nearby park bench, I heard a crack and knew his spine was disabled—for now.

Knowing there was no choice, I lunged my muzzle into his chest, instinct took hold and, he became my first victim. The taste was satisfying—to the hunger I knew to be insatiable.

I was now in a world I despised, with no escape.

I left nothing behind, only bones. The sun was just hours away and the cop cruiser still contained frightened officers.

After I was fed, I felt better, and my body retracted slowly and painfully back to its human state. I was naked, exposed, and covered in blood—mostly my own, but my legs had finally healed.

"Jax?" Kyle crowed from the hole in the roof.

"Are you alright?" I asked.

"Ugh, I'm fine. It's you we're worried about," he confessed.

"I don't understand it, you need to lock me up before it happens again," I ordered.

"Get in the car," Kyle insisted. His guard was down now that I was human and in my rawest form. He tossed me his jacket and I covered myself as best I could.

Tears streamed from my face, but as I wiped them with my hands, the fluid thick and sticky—I realized it was blood.

I gazed into the rear-view mirror as we approached the station and realized my face was in pieces. It looked as if a poorly educated aesthetician had butchered my face tearing holes in my skin. Blood was congealing in the small cavities and with every movement of my face, came a sharp sting.

But it didn't stop there. My hands ached with what I imagined arthritis to be, my feet felt as though I'd just had cortisone injections in them. Every muscle felt like it was reanimating, and it hurt like a *bitch*.

Kyle and the other deputies helped me from the car, escorting me into the station. They didn't hesitate to lock me in a cell.

I hoped they'd throw away the key.

This was no life, I knew that. I knew the pain a life like this could cause. I had seen that pain in Lupe's eyes daily as she dragged herself from her bed each morning. She wouldn't want this, and I certainly didn't.

"You're gonna have to hang out in here for a while until I can figure out what happened, Jax." Kyle sighed.

"No. You can't release me…ever!" I hissed through the bars.

"I can't hold you here, you know that!" He argued.

"But I killed someone!" I scowled.

"No. You killed *something*…" he huffed.

"You know what I can become, Kyle. You've got to see sense, man!" I yelled.

"I have a job to do, and right now I have three officers being rushed to Columbia Hospital, a suspect going to Astoria Animal Hospital, and another two going to OHSU. I will hold you for the day, then I'm cutting you loose," Kyle finished.

I buried my face in my hands, grabbing the wet towelette he handed me to wipe my face with along with a pile of old clothes from the lost and found.

"Thanks," I scoffed.

The towelette was cold and barely wet, nowhere wet enough to wipe away the drying blood.

I flung it to the corner and gave up. I pulled on the spare clothes and tossed Kyle's borrowed jacket back through the bars.

The station cells were cold, quiet, and absent of any other offenders. Down the hall, I could hear anarchy unfolding in the office reception as calls came in from EMS to report on the officers on duty. I could hear every phone call with superior hearing despite the distance to my holding cell. Emergency staff came in to help and the clacking of shoes on the floorboards quickly picked up.

The day drifted away slowly as I sat in my cell and the buzzing found its calm. The phones ceased their incessant ringing and the footwork slowed as patrols went out to conduct interviews to question anyone who could give them any form of assistance.

Nightfall began to roll in and Kyle returned to the station. I hadn't slept still; I was too busy torturing myself with ideas of what I'd do to any other werewolf who crossed my path.

"Time to go, Jax," Kyle announced as he opened the cell door.

"You're making a big mistake…" I groaned.

"I don't have the authority to keep you, friend or not," Kyle sighed.

"Lie then!" I pressed.

"Unless you want to end up in a laboratory under a scalpel with someone running tests on you, you'll do as I say!" He grabbed my wrist and pulled me forward.

I was in no hurry to get out of here, I was in no hurry for anything, but I knew Kyle was right. If anyone knew what I was capable of, I'd never see daylight again.

But I had nothing to go back to, no Lupe and Joel, my hospital was on *fire* the last time I saw it.

Words failed me as I tried to wave off Kyle, but nothing followed. No expression, no gesture—I was just numb, and from the sad eyes Kyle threw me, he knew it too.

I pushed my way through the door, my body feeling different, more powerful—but with a constant *ache*.

I knew there was a war raging within me—one I couldn't win. The beast had already won—it had already stolen so much from me.

I walked all the way home, barefoot, with the stench of thieves and drug addicts dripping from my *borrowed* clothes, only slightly masked by the heavy rainfall, rainfall as heavy as the evening I first met Lupe.

Suddenly, there I was, standing on the road between our two homes not knowing which direction to take.

Both homes had nothing to offer me now. Not my little brother and his excessive drinking, nor Lupe and those foul frozen dinners.

I was alone, lonelier than I'd ever been before.

I stood on the road for quite some time, just to feel something other than guilt, as the rain pelted down upon me, disguising my tears, absorbing my pain as it washed the blood from my body.

Finally, I turned to my left… to Lupe's home. I found the front door unlocked and the back door still flailing in the brisk air. The BBQ was still on the counter and a pie lie face down on the floor of the kitchen.

'The TV was still on as I tried to imagine the seconds that lead to this.

Could I have stopped it? Could I have saved them? I knew there was no point punishing myself like this, but what else was I going to do?

My skin was hot and flushed, even in the cold air. Lupe had left the windows wide open as usual.

I grabbed a towel from the cupboard and dragged myself down the hallway to her ensuite bathroom to shower. It still smelt of her sweet fruity shower gels and candles. Her room was a mess, and there were still boxes upon boxes of books. I guess it was up to me now to clean this all up.

The shower filled the en-suite with steam as it billowed out from behind the curtain. My skin was healing slowly, faster than normal but the red dots and new stretch marks on my skin were still extremely noticeable.

Once I was done in the shower, I finally laid down on Lupe's bed. It was like sleeping on a cloud, not because of how it felt, but how it *smelt*. It smelt of her and I never wanted to leave this feeling of home. My eyes were sore and heavy, my stomach disgustingly *full*. I'd ingested something I wasn't proud of, but gratefully it had stayed my hunger.

V.J.Garland

Chapter Two

Jax

I woke early the next morning.

For what I'd endured over the last few days—I slept rather well. I didn't feel the beast stirring within me and prayed it never would again.

I planned to clean up Lupe's house today. Tomorrow, my own. I'd pack up some stuff and never come back. I couldn't see myself living here any longer. I couldn't see myself anywhere at all. The future was a dismal blur.

There was a knock at the door, and I went to answer it.

Through the large glass windows, I could see a sheriff's uniform. It was Kyle. I opened the door without a sound or greeting.

"Jax, I tried you over at your place…" he started and trailed off as I interrupted.

"I haven't been there yet," I groaned.

"I get it, Jax. Take your time with this. Do you need any help?" he offered as he handed me a paper cup full of hot coffee.

"Come in…" I said as I sat on the sofa.

"What can I do?" he asked softly.

"I don't even know where to begin, Kyle," I huffed over a sip of coffee.

"Start small, with small belongings, there's no rush to empty the place," he said encouragingly.

"It's just being here, without them. Not knowing what's instore for me, what if I turn again?" I whispered.

"I'm here for you, man. Whatever you need," He grabbed my shoulder softly.

"How is everything out there?" I asked.

"Ugh, you know…the media want answers, there's a lot of blood on this town right now. We lost some good people," he sniffed.

"And they deserve answers…" I grunted.

"You aren't responsible for all that. You saved us, you never once looked at me as your next meal," he sympathized.

"There was a bigger meal to be had, we probably just got lucky, don't bet on that happening again," I urged.

"Where will you go?" He asked.

"Hadn't even thought about it to be honest," I confessed.

"Need some company?" Kyle asked with a smile.

"You don't want to be what I am, Kyle. It's a pain you can never shake," I explained.

"No, I don't want to be like you, we can look out for each other, like back in kinder," he snickered.

"Looking out for you getting wedgies was one thing, stopping myself from eating you is entirely different," I grinned.

"Nonetheless, you could use the distraction, if I start to annoy you, I'll come home," he edged.

"Let me think about it, I've got two houses to organize and clear before I do anything," I sighed.

"Ever the responsible, even after what you've been through," he sipped his coffee.

"I better get to the station, I'll drop by tonight," he finished as he stood up and walked out the front door.

I skulled the remainder of the coffee and huffed as I looked about the house, where would I even begin.

I paced the floors for a second as I decided what I was going to do. There were only two rooms in use, the main bedroom, and the bathroom in that room. If I cleared them first, I'd only have the kitchen and lounge to worry about it.

The piles of books were easy, I had this superhuman strength that made 30 books feel like 1, the hardest part was packing up her clothes, she didn't have too many so that was hardly the challenge, it was the nostalgia and memories of her in them.

Amongst her drawers, I found notebooks—and diaries.

She had kept a log of Noah's life as a werewolf, of her life living in the misery.

Lupina's Letters

Dear Monday,

It's been a while since I logged my life. It's gotten pretty interesting lately.

Noah and I just bought a house, we came to the cabin to celebrate and do some hunting. He'd promised the firehouse a months' worth of meat. Christian popped down for a day with Elouise, and that's as much fun as we've had so far.

Lupe x

Oh Saturday,

Noah's been unwell, cold sweats and high fevers, we'll see how he is over the next day. We might be calling our trip short, but we'll be back.

Lupe x

Tuesday,

Things got weird today, Noah must have been sleepwalking. I found him out in the field, he'd been coughing up blood. His hands were covered in it, and his fever has caused some sort of skin allergy. I've called a doctor. I don't think he'll be well enough to travel. Hopefully they make the call by morning. He's irritable and not really himself.

Lupe x

Friday,

I wish I could explain what's happened, but I feel winded. That absent minded feeling of what would happen if the world was ending, but you know it isn't, so you stop worrying. My worry has been constant, it feels like at least my world is ending. Noah attacked me today, his face changed into something dark and horrifying, his hands reached for me, but they weren't his hands. Then like a flash he was back. I can't explain it.

Lupe x

Monday,

El called today, Christian was concerned that Noah hadn't come into work. I'd been forced to lie to my best friend. Noah wasn't safe to be around. I found him passed out dawn on the driveway with the corpse of some animal next to him, he had mauled it down to the bone, so much so that I couldn't recognize what kind of animal it was.

It's for the best that everyone thinks we've moved away, so I strung together a lie that I got a position at a Publishing House in Portland. At least for now.

Lupe x

Dear Diary,

I don't know what to do. I'm afraid. But I'm in too deep now. How can something turn from perfect to anarchy overnight?

Lupe x

It's the 4th of July today,

We'd let our phones die and shutoff the power to the house. I ran the necessities from a petrol generator. I tried to stay as out of touch as possible from everyone we knew in order to keep them safe.

I couldn't recall the last time Noah slept, he spends all his time pacing the field or in the bathroom. I started keeping a calendar, marking it when he fully turned. The first night was frightening. He made me lock myself in the basement and then lock myself in the cellar for added measure. It didn't take him long to break through the main door. But I'm still here. . .Barely, for now... Lupe x

August,

Noah's begged me to leave him, but I can't. I can't let him battle this alone, if there's anyway, I want to be there to help him. I can't give up that easily. But I'm fighting a losing battle, we both are. . .

Lupe x

December,

I tasted it today, Noah flung a chunk of flesh at me. I wanted to see if my accepting his ways would ease his brutality towards me. So, I reach out and grabbed the lump of meat and pressed it to my face. Then I saw the remains of what could only have been a tattoo as I turned it to examine what it was or where it came from. The vomiting was immediate. But nothing came up. I was running on empty. I knew in the back of my mind what he had been doing, but I'd never seen him bring it back here. In my head I told myself it was only animals, but I knew better. I was physically ill for days. The mental effects were worse, I kept waking suddenly, the memory of the taste would replay over my tastebuds, the same way you think you smell your grandmothers baking, but it's your mind playing tricks on you. I want it to end. I need it to end.

Lupe

May,

Noah's doing better, and by better, I mean he hasn't tried to kill me in a while. He's kept his murderous business outside and I've managed to reclaim some parts of the house. He's barely inside anymore. He's given me that much. But he's barely there now, it's just her. The beast that controls him, I've taken to referring to it as a woman, only a woman could be this heinous and vicious. Our world had been infected by her; she'd stolen him from me.

Lupe x

November,

Sorry memories, it's been longer and longer between entries. There isn't much to tell these days. I'm still here at the cabin. Noah hasn't turned back into his full human form for over a month, he lurks around intimidatingly, sometimes I wonder why he doesn't just kill me. Maybe he's afraid to be alone? That's how I feel all the time, I feel like the world forgot about us. Well, it did because I told it to...

Lupe x

December Christmas day,

It's snowing outside, it's the most beautiful thing I've seen in a long time. I strolled outside trying to adopt some habit, testing Noah to how far he'd let me go alone. He let me go to the store, but small stores and he watched me like prey. He glared from the porch stairs bare chested in the cold, his face inhibited by sores and the look of agony. I wanted to help him, to touch him. Being so close but so helpless was a pain worse than anything she could do to me. I guess you don't realize how much you love someone until you're faced with exactly what kind of sacrifice you need to make for them.

I cooked two microwave meals for lunch, picked some winter pansies and placed them on the table.

I couldn't lose another Christmas to this chaos, but I knew that was unreasonable thinking.

He came inside and sat at the table with me. We hadn't done this in months, maybe years? I'd lost track of how long we'd been like this. His eyes were glowing, yellow, puffy, dark and red. He was worn.

"You know I can't eat this Lupe," he growled in his raspy voice. I hadn't heard him speak in a long time; his voice was harsher, deeper.

"Please just try," I begged. Tears flooded my face; I couldn't bring the food to my mouth.

His eyes softened, but just for a moment. Then it was rage.

"I didn't choose this!" He stormed outside and come near me since. I wonder if he reads this. If you do Noah, let me back in.

Lupe

August,

I can't take back the evil I've committed. And I'm broken for it... I'm sorry, I'm barely surviving.

Lupe

Noah,

I can't keep going, I know you're in there somewhere. But can we make it out alive... together?

Lupe

Lupe,

I know you meant forever. You've proven that 1000 times over. I'm trying to come back to you. Wait for me . . .

Noah xo

Noah,

I'm selfish cause I can't let you go, you're my person. Tell me what to do...

Lupe x

My Dear Lupina,

I'm so deeply sorry for the life we've led these past years. For the violence you've witnessed, for the part you've played in keeping your vows to me. But we can't continue this way I've drained more life from you than all the people I've killed combined. I don't know how this happened, but I don't wish for it to burden your life further. Forget this was ever our life, forget about me. Use this money to get your life back, find yourself an apartment, get the cat you always wanted, and a well-paying job.

I'll love you always,

Noah

Dear Diary,

He left, I don't know if I'm elated or completely shattered. It's been a week and he hasn't come home. He's really gone. I have no more tears; I don't even know what the tears really meant. I've been alone for so long, but the presence is what I miss. It's time to get up and start again. So goodbye diary, it's time to close this chapter of my life. Wish me luck!

Lupe x

I was glad nobody was around; I could barely stitch together any reasonable thought.

I'd been mad, thinking he kept her as his plaything, to torture and torment, but she really did want to stay and simply love him, even if that love wasn't the same as it once was. Lupe was the perfect example of a woman committed.

I needed to figure out a way to survive. Already, some knew about me and what I was capable of. I'd have to leave, they'd be after me soon, if not planning it already.

The thought of ringing my parents felt like someone was crushing my chest, they'd been estranged from him for years, they didn't approve of his wild nature, they didn't approve of anything unless it made a quick buck and set you amongst the elite. Now didn't feel like the right time, there wasn't one, so I pushed the thought away and concentrated on the task at hand.

I pressed on with packing Lupe's belongings and had it done in record time, everything fit into six big boxes. Her one pot and two pans included. The rest of the furniture belonged to the house.

Her more personal belongings were stuffed in her backpack; she wasn't a handbag kind of a woman. Her wallet was old, sleek, and stuffed with loose change that had softened the leather from wear and tear, the rest was crushed up dollar bills, her license was out of date by years and still had an old address on it from where she originally lived in Chico. There were old bank letters for late payments to an address outside Red Bluff and a bunch of restaurant menus from here in Warrenton.

The thought occurred to me that I didn't really need to clean out my own house of Joel's belongings, not yet at least. I was mortgage-free three years ago and had no overheads forcing me to make rash decisions.

I carted the boxes over to my house and stashed them in the oversized garage.

Lupe's bag I placed on the kitchen counter as I sipped at a bottle of aged whiskey.

My hands were red and sore, the skin crisp and dry with cracks running deep where the callused skin was after erupting with death daggers. My jaw was achy, and my eyes stung every time I blinked.

After wallowing my way to the bottom of the bottle I sat in a hot shower before composing myself to pack a bag and skip town, but I had no idea where I would go, I drew on the steamed glass a map of the USA and willed myself to find a getaway, I always hit California. My business with Lupe wasn't over, she deserved a clean slate—her family and friends deserved closure.

I yanked myself from the shower, annoyingly far soberer than I wanted to be and a loud bang crashed on my front door.

"Hold on!" I shouted as I wrestled a towel around my waist.

I opened the door, and it was Celinde, Kyle, and Carrie.

"What are you all doing here?" I questioned.

"There's a warrant out for you. We know what we saw, we are here to show support," Celinde blurted.

She and Carrie were the two paramedics from the beach.

"Forget that, I'm leaving," I sighed.

"They'll find you," Carrie huffed.

"They have to catch me first," I growled.

"But you're innocent, you might be one of those things, but you saved our lives, you never hurt anyone," Kyle pressed.

They pushed their way into the house, closed the door behind them and made themselves comfortable at the kitchen bench on the stools as Kyle poured water for everyone.

"If you run you look guilty, they can plant this whole thing on you," Carrie argued.

"If I don't, they'll chain me up in a lab and run experiments on me for the rest of my life," I argued back.

"He has a point, they wouldn't just let him walk knowing what he is," Kyle agreed.

"There's more out there…" Celinde sighed.

"I'll kill any I come across," I nodded.

"You'd kill your own kind?" She enquired.

"Kill or be killed, once they know I won't harm humans they aren't likely to welcome me with a hug," I snuffed.

"How do you know you can control yourself," Carrie questioned.

I ran my hand over Lupe's bag and her memory washed over me, her tenderness and hope.

"I owe it to Lupe and Noah…" I sighed.

"Who's Noah?" Kyle asked curiously.

"Lupe's husband, it's complicated but I think he was the first, the beginning," I grumbled.

"How do you know?" Carrie asked.

"I read some of Lupe's diaries," I confessed.

"Bad!" Celinde scolded teasingly.

"I had to know more, it's not like I can just ask her," I sighed as I felt a puddle building in the corner of my eye.

I walked back to my room and shut the door behind me as I dressed in jeans, a plain black t-shirt, and a bomber jacket. I stuffed my bag with medical supplies, clothes, shoes, and all the cash I had put away in my safe.

This was it, I had to leave my comfortable lifestyle behind. I carried the two big duffle bags out to the kitchen and stashed some food in the emptier one.

"I'm coming with you…" Kyle announced.

"You can't, you'll just get in the way," I sighed.

"I don't care, I've followed you most of my life Jax, we do this together. Whatever it is you need to do—I'll have your back," he patted me on the shoulder and a half-smile smoldered over his face.

"I appreciate you," I smiled as I rested my hand on his forearm still attached to my shoulder.

"Hell, I'm in too," Celinde grinned.

"Not like we have jobs here anymore, I'm in too," Carrie smiled.

"You guys realize I'm not relocating, I'm not going on holiday, you'll be accessories," I explained.

"What is your infinite goal in this?" Carrie asked.

"I'm going to kill every werewolf I can find, and then try to find some peace," I exhaled.

"Already got my rifle in the truck," Kyle chuckled.

"This won't be easy, it'll be rough, you're in constant danger with me, I don't expect this of any of you," I pressed.

"Jax, we get it. We're coming with you regardless," Carrie hugged me tightly and Celinde followed. It wasn't the hug I wanted but it was the one I needed.

I felt the pang of pain in my chest, the pain of knowing I would never see or hear Joel's voice again, there'd be no more inappropriate comments during grocery shopping, no more missing wine bottles or steak cooking at 3 am as he tried to impress his latest catch.

This small group of friends was willing to put themselves on the line and I struggled to understand why, but they were all individuals with nothing to go home to, no jobs, no lovers, just endless nights. And that's what brought us together.

Chapter Three

Jax

We loaded ourselves into Kyle's Jeep and stopped off at everyone's homes to pack a bag. The boot was loaded with duffle bags, guns, and Lupe's diaries.

"Jax, I forgot to tell you earlier, Lupina's ashes are ready for pickup, I ordered them to be rushed," Kyle hesitated.

A deep sigh washed over me once again and I composed myself as best I could.

"That's actually perfect, we should take them to her family," I nodded.

"Where to?" Kyle asked.

"Butte county... Chico," I replied.

"You girls ready for this?" Kyle questioned, giving them a gentle opportunity to reconsider.

"Let's hit it!" Carrie smiled.

We stopped at the funeral home first and Kyle went in to collect the ashes.

"Do you want to hold this?" he slowly inched it toward me, unsure if that were the right move.

"I'm not ready for that…" I shut my eyes tight and turned away.

"Here, I'll take care of her," Celinde held out her hands and tucked the urn into her backpack.

"It'll get better Jax," she squeezed my shoulder from behind me and my callused hand held hers.

The drive was 9 hours from here and Kyle made it in 6, the girls slept through most of it out of fear, but we approached slowly as Kyle asked for directions for where to go.

We stopped at the address on the bank statement first, but it was empty and seemingly untouched for years. The lawn was a field of long green grass, the mailbox was crammed full of mail and the windows were water damaged and crusted with dirt.

If you didn't judge it from the wear and tear it was a beautiful home, somewhere I could imagine a happy Lupe… Happy Lupe, I'd rarely seen that side of her.

"Any other ideas?" Celinde yawned.

"Fire station, Noah was a firefighter. They might know something," I nodded.

We all piled back into the car and headed a few streets away till we saw the firehouse.

There were four men out the front running drills and others cleaning the trucks.

Celinde jumped out of the jeep first with Lupe's urn in her hands.

"I'll take her..." I sighed.

I approached the men running drills and they were quick to stop and introduce themselves.

Hi, I'm Jax, I'm looking for directions to a relative of an ex-employee from here?" I began.

"I'm Rick, who's the person you're looking for?" he asked as he shook my hand.

"It's complex, I'm a friend of Lupina's, her husband was Noah," but before I finished the sentence the shorter of them had seen the writing on the urn and dropped to the floor.

"Is that what I think it is?" another croaked through a shattered voice.

"Unfortunately," Kyle said, holding my shoulder tight once more.

"Come inside bro, Christian is the man to see," Rick sighed.

We walked into the main room where others were sitting eating, Rick approached another man with dark hair, a mustache, and kind look about him.

He dashed over to me and picked up the urn from my hands and collapsed to the floor.

His eyes flooded quickly and just as fast looked to me for answers.

"Where's Noah?" he begged.

"I'm sorry man, he didn't make it," I sighed.

The outcry was piercing and stirred the pain in me harder knowing and feeling the love in this house for them both.

"Do you know where Lupe's family is?" Carrie asked softly.

"It was just her mom. She passed about 3 years ago now. We didn't know how to reach Lupe. Noah has no family either; we were his family." Christian cried.

Celinde made herself comfortable in the kitchen and was fixing coffee for everyone while Carrie passed them out.

Kyle never left my side; he was afraid something would set me off and I'd rip this whole house to shreds. But I felt a deeper sense of control.

"What happened?" Christian asked.

"I couldn't tell you, but she can," I dropped the diary on the table and Christian began reading through pages and pages of agony. His eyes welled up in disbelief and then in sorrow.

"This can't be true? It's impossible," his eyes darted to me.

"I thought so too…" I sighed. I flexed my hands softly and allowed him a glimpse of my claws.

"What the fuck!" he jumped back into Rick.

"I won't hurt you," I sighed.

"Well, that's debatable…" Kyle interjected with sarcasm.

"Not the time," Carrie hissed from the kitchen. She helped herself to a cup of hot tea and biscuits.

"Can I see," Christian asked curiously as he slowly moved back in.

"Sure," I held out my hand and let him examine me.

"Did you know Noah?" He asked.

"I was there when he died, I hadn't met him before that. Lupe moved to Warrenton after he left her, we became friends and we almost started dating when he and his pack showed up and turned on each other, none of them survived but I got nicked by someone's claw in the fight... must have been what turned me," I sighed.

"I'm sorry for your loss, Lupe was one of a kind. She did a number on Noah when they first met," He smiled at the thought of them together.

"She was special, even after all they went through, she had nothing but good things to say about Noah," I smiled.

"He was my best friend," he sobbed.

"I'll avenge him and put a stop to this madness, I promise you," our foreheads touched, and his hand was hard against my shoulder blade.

"Take me with you...I can help," he sniffed.

"You don't mean that, you have a life here," I tried to brush him off.

"No, I don't. My girlfriend left me for another guy and I'm just living for my job now, give me some purpose. Let me make Noah's life meaningful again," his eyes didn't leave mine and before I could say anything Kyle had piped up again.

"We got one seat left, it's yours," Kyle had sad soggy eyes as he watched on.

"But you have a home here, there's no home where we are going, just blood, pain and chaos..." I confessed sorely.

"I won't pretend to know any amount of what I'm walking into," He sighed.

"You are walking into darkness, there is no light where we are going, you might very well die." I expressed as I caught a glimpse of Carrie comforting Celinde.

He thought for a moment, looking between the faces in the room. Rick was a clammy mixture of white and green, he was awash with grief and the urge to vomit, I'd felt that way once too.

"What does it taste like?" he questioned.

"What do you mean?" I queried curiously.

"Taking a life?" he pressed.

"It tastes like sadness and desperation…" I choked.

"You don't need to play any role in that, you don't even have to come. You can pretend we never came here and carry-on living." I urged.

"Just because you can, doesn't mean you should. I'm with you, Jax." He smiled softly as he stood from the chair.

He wasn't as tall as Noah, perhaps 6"1 maybe slightly shorter, athletic build and that Super Mario look about him.

"Give me a day to clear out my stuff," he nodded to Kyle.

"Sure man," Kyle shook his hand.

Celinde and Carrie took the jeep and bought lunch for everyone, most were chatty, but they all kept a close eye on me along with extra distance. I wasn't offended, I was content in my quiet corner. I clutched the urn like I was holding Lupe's body for the last time, the last time I had control of it. I knew I had to leave her here, I knew she was in safe hands in this place with people who knew her and would celebrate her for who she was before devastation and turmoil consumed her world.

Carrie walked over with a subway sandwich and a bottle of lemonade.

"Here, you look like you could use this," she said with her husky voice.

"Thanks, Carrie,".

"Jax, that stuff you said to Christian about darkness and dying?" She started to say.

"Carrie, that's all possible. I don't know what waits for me, all I know is you are in danger even being in my presence," I interrupted.

"But it seems so dormant, maybe you beat it," she said with a small skip to her voice.

"I wish, but the beast inside me is asleep, not dead," I sighed.

Her eyes sunk as she accepted my words and she slumped into the sofa beside me and put one hand over mine on the urn.

"Thanks for being here," I whispered.

"It's gonna take all four of us to look out for you," she snickered.

"And one of me to keep you alive," I chuckled back.

"How will we find the rest like you?" she questioned.

"Follow the trail of death and destruction, Lupe had been tracking news reports of mass murders up in Washington till they hit Oregon, that's when she spilled the beans and decided to try and find Noah," I explained.

"And that wasn't such a good idea…" Carrie sighed.

"Joel and more so Lupe saved a lot of people, if Lupe hadn't of killed Noah, we'd all be dead," I grunted.

"What? She killed him?" she gasped.

"He made her do it, I don't know how she did it, but it was as if he let her. He'd taken a huge attack that should have killed him, but the final blow came from Lupe and when he died the rest of his pack slowly became clouds of ash," Her hand held mine tighter around Lupe.

"How did she die?" Carrie was invested in every word by now.

"The pole she ran through his heart—he fell onto her, and that same pole crushed her sternum, Noah was huge, I tried to pull him off, but I couldn't, and then she was all that was left covered in his remains. Lights and sirens were flashing and wailing and before I knew it Kyle was pulling me off them. Joel, Noah, all of them were mounds of dark debris. Joel's body was lost to the wind," Carrie's eyes were teary and Celinde had sat down to listen also.

"We'll clean up this mess, any werewolf left, will be dealt with," Celinde was fierce and overly confident.

"Well, we better prepare ourselves. Food supplies, weapons, it would help if we knew any weaknesses, Jax?" Carrie asked.

"I haven't been one long enough to notice anything yet. Afraid I'm not much help there," I sighed.

"Catch!" Yelled Christian.

He hurled a silver bracelet at me, and I caught it with ease.

"Silver? Original…" I laughed.

"So, nothing," he questioned.

"I feel the same," I replied.

"Heads!" Kyle called as he threw a bulb of garlic at me.

"Garlic is for vampires you idiot," I threw the bulb back at him.

"You just never know…" he huffed.

"Christian, you got any silver nitrate around here?" Celinde asked.

"Yeah, there'll be some in the vans," he answered as he walked towards the doors to the vans.

"So, we're just going to test random substances on me now?" I grunted with a furrowed brow.

"Wish there was an easier way bro," Kyle snickered slightly excited, he always was a big science nerd.

"So do I," I sighed as Celinde walked in with a tube of silver nitrate applicators.

"Maybe you should sit down for this," she urged.

Christian, Kyle, and two others came to my side and held each of my four limbs down while Celinde ran the nitrate over my arm.

"Anything?" she asked.

"Nothing, make a small scratch and try?" I suggested.

"You're sure?" she sqeaked.

"We're here now, let's get it done." I huffed.

Carrie brought over a sharp knife and ran it over my forearm and Celinde stuck the applicator right into the open wound.

"Well, no bubbling, no steam… he's calm. This was a failure," Carrie announced.

"Steam? Really," I chuckled.

"There's got to be something else we can try!" Carrie groaned.

"Try the bracelet again," Christian suggested.

Celinde ran the chain through the gash, but there was nothing. No point, no discomfort just the wound slowly closing and the blood reabsorbing back into my skin.

"What about colloidal silver? There are actual silver particles in it," I suggested.

"Christian?" Carrie asked hinting at his knowledge of the inventory.

"Here's some," Rick shouted from the first aid cupboard.

"Ready?" Kyle asked.

"Just get it over with," I squinted my eyes shut tight.

I felt the droplets hit my skin and the immediate burn raged through my forearm.

"Ahh! Fuck!" I yelled.

"Okay, we got something!" Celinde cried in joy.

Rick rushed over with bandages and tried to prevent the silver from penetrating further, but it was already bone-deep, and my supersonic healing was having trouble keeping up.

"That's incredible…" he said completely mystified.

I looked down to my forearm to see what was so amusing while I sat writhing in pain. My skin was burnt black but still fighting back, a patch of fur formed, and I felt the bristly hair sprouts forcing out the silver and ripping through my skin. They felt sharp and barbed and barely less painful than the colloidal itself.

"Dude…." Kyle was gazing and forgetting to blink as he looked on with Rick.

"We got bubbles!" Kyle squeaked.

"Those aren't bubbles, it's oozing," Celinde gasped.

"Get it off of me!" I groaned in pain.

"Holy water?" Kyle chuckled.

"Not the time!" I sprung up from my seat and launched myself into the kitchen desperately washing it off under cold water.

"Is that working?" Carrie asked.

I looked down, the wound was closing and the hairs began retracting as hard tiny marbles of silver death escaped my body.

"Luckily," I nodded.

"Well, at least we have a weapon now," Carrie smiled.

"How? Water pistols," I smirked.

"Hose?" Christian beamed.

"Huh?" Celinde chimed.

"We have an old fire truck around the back just rusting, it still runs, just needs an oil change and some gas, it's just an ornament collecting dust to us," Rick announced.

"How much you want for it?" I asked.

"Just buy us dinner," he smiled.

"Done! Let's go check it out," I was excited, as much as I liked the jeep, it was a squeeze and now with Christian in tow, we'd be struggling for room for any belongings at all.

Rick and three others lead us around the back and of the house and there stood a tanker no more than ten years old.

"It's commonly known as a triple, has a water tank, hose, and it can pump water. What you choose to put in the tank is entirely up to you…" he smiled at Carrie.

"You mean we could put colloidal silver in there?" she gleamed, she was fully invested in this and Celinde was busying herself with a young engineer looking through a pizza menu.

"Christian, can that be done?" Rick asked.

"Nobody's ever tried it but it's nonacidic, I don't see why not," he agreed.

"So where do we get that much colloidal silver?" I asked.

"You're the Doctor, shouldn't you know," Kyle smacked me on the back with encouragement.

"Amazon!" Carrie suggested.

"Okay, Celinde's already on dinner it seems. Christian, should we warm this baby up and see what she can still do?" I asked.

"Let's do it," Ricked tossed him a set of keys.

"I'll go see if we can get a next-day delivery," Carrie said as she began to walk back to the firehouse.

Christian was in the truck turning the ignition and three other guys brought out large containers of oil.

"I need to offer you my thanks, you do not need to be this generous or understanding of my situation," I said as my head dropped.

"We're all in this for Noah, bro, think nothing of it," Christian smiled.

"He would have liked you," Christian smiled as he opened the window.

"How do you know? I kinda stole his girl," I laughed.

"Because I like you! Unique circumstances, he'd have been happy there was someone taking care of her, as lovely as she was, she wasn't much of a cook. They ate here almost every night," he laughed at the fondness of the memory.

"Sounds like the Lupe I know," I chuckled along.

"They were good people; I know you probably know nothing about Noah or very little. He was the guy who would greet you with a strong handshake, a warm hug and, a cold beer even if he didn't know you. Never passed judgment on others, very compassionate soul," he sighed.

"It must have been hard for him to be what I am," I sighed.

"It'll be hard for you too? Did one of the girls call you a doctor?" he questioned.

"Ahhh. I was the resident surgeon back in Warrenton. Nothing flashy really, just a lot of boat injuries, odd amputation," I tried to be humble about it.

"So, helping people is in your blood too," He smiled.

"I guess so," I agreed.

"Jax!" Celinde yelled.

I strolled over towards her as she handed me a large pepperoni pizza and a bottle of pop.

"Thanks," I smiled.

"So, he's riding with us?" she blushed as she looked over my shoulder at Christian as he poured oil into the truck.

"You can ride in there with him if you like," I smiled.

She blushed again and inhaled a breath of confidence as she went to talk to him.

I didn't know much about Celinde, but I'd never heard of her having a boyfriend, that kind of news spreads down hospital hallways faster than a power surge. She was 24yrs old—a baby really, but with a good head on her shoulders. Her admission paperwork was always perfect and highly detailed, Carrie on the other hand was slightly scrappy, she had this urgency about her with a powerful presence to boot. Celinde was the calm. Her appearance was softer, dark blonde hair almost chestnut with an olive skin tone and dark brown eyes, she stood about 5'6 and had an athletic build.

Carrie was a little shorter, she had vibrant copper hair with ringlet curls that hugged her pale face well and hazel-colored eyes. She was also athletically built, but with a slightly rounded rump. She had a reputation and Kyle had long been the guy she couldn't hook after many failed attempts.

I sat down at the table with Carrie as she ordered items from Amazon with one hand and devoured a folded slice of pizza in the other. Kyle brought over drinks for us, and the engineer Dave came and joined us.

"Thanks for having us here," I nodded.

"It's nice to have some excitement around here, Chico is a pretty boring place in the winter. If you guys want to get some sleep, we have a whole room full of spare beds, help yourselves to some pillows and blankets," he smiled.

"I appreciate that, thank you for your hospitality," I nodded.

"How are you getting on there, Carebear," Kyle asked.

"All done, we have thousands of dollars' worth of Colloidal on the way and sleeping bags, long life food, toilet paper, and nerf water guns," she grinned.

"What do I owe you?" I asked.

"My life savings, but don't worry, you can get the next one," she smiled.

"Do you guys have any idea what you're looking for? People don't just stumble off down the highway and come across werewolves…" Dave laughed.

"Lupe was tracking Noah through the news and smaller outlets that weren't so loud about massacres, assuming they didn't want to invite bad publicity and lose out on tourism, but what happened up at Hurricane was too big to bury, what most big outlets failed to report were the smaller crimes. There's been a string of violent murders that kind of trailed Noah's pack, but they seemed to split off on their own, it's still active so whatever killed Noah and Joel didn't kill them," I sighed.

"Different pack, maybe the connection is what bound their fates?" Carrie asked puzzled.

"It seems that way," I sighed.

"But there was conflict amongst the pack, isn't that why this all went pear-shaped in the first place?" Kyle asked.

"Conflict, but they hadn't parted yet. Maybe that's how werewolves set themselves apart," I thought out loud.

"So where do we find this new pack?" Carrie asked.

"Portland," I sighed.

"That's so populated!" she huffed.

"That's probably why they are there, it's hardly any work for them, all you can eat buffet," Dave added.

"Well, I guess we'll head there once we have all our supplies ready," Carrie mumbled through her pizza.

Celinde and Christian walked through the doors, they seemed to have hit it off already. She was smiling and he was laughing, and I felt a warmth of happiness for them. While it wasn't anything right now, I'd just be happy if someone found anything good from this disaster.

"Let's get some sleep guys," Kyle yawned.

The hours had ticked over quickly, and Christian went to empty his locker and began saying goodbye to everyone at the station. I hoped one day I could return him safely, in a week, a month or whenever he felt ready to come home, but he didn't seem like he'd miss anything here other than the people.

Carrie and Celinde were making beds for everyone and fluffing pillows, Kyle had gone to take a shower and I sat clutching Lupe's diary once again. There was so much hope in here, so much fuel for me to rectify this for her.

"Come on, Jax. You need to get some rest!" Celinde ordered.

"Yeah, you're right," I peeled the blankets back and cocooned myself into a bed. My eyes were heavy immediately and I drifted off.

Chapter Four

Jax

Carrie's Amazon order had arrived at 8 am, Christian was in the kitchen making breakfast for the new shift of workers and had briefly explained why we were here. They were a tight-knit crew, nobody hesitated to tell their truths.

Kyle and Celinde were dumping all the colloidal into the tank of the triple while Carrie and I packed the food into the jeep. I'd been ordered to stay far away from the triple encase of a leak or spill and after that tiny droplet yesterday I had no objections. My skin still felt slightly tighter in that spot.

"Well, that's all done! We're ready when you guys are," Kyle smiled as he wiped the beads of sweat from his forehead.

"Who's riding with who?" Kyle asked.

"I'll go with Christian in the triple... if that's okay?" Celinde smiled.

"Go ahead!" Carrie smiled back.

"Cool, Jax, Carrie and me will take the jeep. I still have a radio, when we get closer, we can listen in for any activity," Kyle added.

"Genius! Why didn't you mention that before?" I laughed.

"The same reason I didn't make it through law school, I'm not that bright," he chuckled.

We all erupted in laughter at his joke and seconds behind him was Christian hauling out a box of beer.

"I feel like we'll be needing this," he gleamed.

"Yes! You can sit right next to me," Carrie giggled as she took the box and packed it into the backseat of the jeep.

"Celinde's going with you!" I smiled.

Christian's face quickly became a blush and he looked over to see her already sitting in the front seat with her window down.

"We'll follow you!" he shouted as he ran for the truck.

"They definitely like each other," Carrie snickered as we all climbed into the jeep.

"Celinde's a nice girl, I hope it goes well for them," Kyle smiled.

"It will! They've got nothing better to do," I laughed.

"How are you feeling, Jax? Do we need to feed you or something?" Kyle asked inquisitively.

"Nah, I don't think so. Normal human food still fills me and satisfies me just fine," I replied.

"You don't wanna stop off at a butcher for some prime rib?" Carrie teased.

"I'll keep the idea in mind," I laughed.

It took us time and plenty of stops but we finally arrived just outside of Portland. By now we were all well acquainted, comfortable, and slightly annoyed with one another's bad habits. I'd dug more poop holes than I'd like to admit and most of them not even for myself. Carrie's taste in long-life, shelf-stable foods wasn't to anyone's liking, but we avoided roadhouses as much as we could unless we needed gas.

But finally, we were here, and Kyle began searching the channels on the radio and the three of us listened in as we combed the streets of suburbia for anything slightly off.

There seemed to be a string of crime flooding Fairview beside Columbia River and so we thought we'd start there. My nose seemed to agree, something didn't smell right there.

"We should find somewhere to sleep," Carrie groaned through a yawn.

"Haven't you slept enough," Kyle joked. He was clearly tired from the long drive even though we'd tried to take shifts.

"There's always time for more sleep! Gee Kyle, you know nothing about women," She teased.

"Eh, explains why I'm single," he laughed.

My eyes caught Carrie's in the rear-view mirror, and she was blushing. My observation here meant nothing but if these two hooked up it would be a recipe for disaster.

Celinde and Christian had pulled into a parking lot at a park to eat while we looked for somewhere to spend the night.

"It's getting darker," Carrie hummed with an annoying tone.

"I know Care, we'll find somewhere soon," I agreed.

Kyle's phone rang, it was Christian.

"There's an RV park a few streets over, we'll set up there. Should be rather empty in the winter," Christian explained.

"Okay, let's meet there," Kyle hung up. Carrie was already looking for directions.

Once we arrived it didn't take long to pitch the budget tents Carrie had ordered from Amazon, Celinde and Carrie went to get dinner from a nearby store while the rest of us tried to make our situation a little more homely.

We unrolled the sleeping bags and brought out the extra blankets and had a fire going just in time for the girls to return with some hot roast dinners.

The containers were huge, and all lined with enormous Yorkshire puddings that were filled with golden goose fat roasted vegetables, lashings of a dark rich gravy, tender roast beef, a broccoli bake with a cheesy white sauce, steamed corn, peas and carrots, and a generous helping of buttery herb-infused stuffing.

Christian brought out the carton of beers and Celinde laid a bag of marshmallows on top of it with chocolate and graham crackers and he smiled up at her.

We all sat around eating our food and sinking our beers as night came down around us. The moon would be full tomorrow night, my first full moon. I wasn't sure what that would mean for me, according to movies and books that was my time to *shine*, to decimate all life within a village, but my hunger reached beyond humans. Human food kept me healthy and strong but if I wanted to fill my cravings, I'd have to be more adventurous.

"Thanks ladies, I'm stuffed," Kyle burped. He'd gotten through about two and a half beers and the entire meal, he was a burly man, law enforcement suited him far more than law could have. He had a kind nature but a threatening look when he scrunched his eyebrows the right way.

"No trouble! Tomorrow might not be so relaxed if my moon phase app is correct," Celinde sighed.

"Jax, how are you holding up? Do you feel different?" She asked.

"No," but that was a lie, I felt like I was about to erupt in fur and fangs and there'd be nothing anyone could do to stop it, so I let them have one more night stress-free without worrying I'd maul them to death as they slept.

The next day was odd, hazy—like a veil was over my eyes the whole time. It was dizzying and made my skin clammy as if the weather were humid.

But it wasn't, it was freezing, it was November in Oregon, and our sleeping bags weren't enough to keep us warm last night, the beer on the other had got us through.

"The guys left some turnout gear in the truck, might be handy to have an extra layer on for whoever is hosing," Christian said to Kyle as he rumbled through the back seat.

"That'll be you!" Celinde smirked.

"You think you can drive that rig?" He teased.

"I can drive an ambulance, I think I can handle that," she smiled.

"And maybe I'd like to see you in full turnout," she chuckled.

"Celinde!" Carrie howled.

"Ughh, first responders…" I laughed.

Kyle was busy listening to the radio, his face serious as he ignored the banter behind him.

"Jax, something just came through on the radio," Kyle whispered.

"What was it?" Christian jumped.

"Three missing persons, since last night," brows were all raised.

"Any description of the victims?" I asked.

"College students out walking their parent's dog at a park. Neighbors of the park heard screams and shouting, then dead silence," He explained.

"Kids never came home, leash was found at a sewer gate," he added.

"Far from here?" Christian asked.

"About 10mins," He answered.

"Think this is something, Jax?" Kyle asked.

"One way to find out I guess…" I sighed. My eyes felt heavier than normal, they were gritty, like I'd had sand thrown in them. This wasn't a good day to be having a bad day.

We all jumped into the vehicles just before nightfall, the others seemed confident enough in me to be around me, but I was far from confident in myself.

The drive there felt bumpier than usual, I felt ill and nauseous.

"Jax, you don't look so good," Carrie observed.

"I think it's the full moon," I said as I put my head between my knees.

"Almost there, bro," Kyle patted me on the back gently and handed me a bottle of water.

But my eyes snapped up in response and I felt my iris pop, I felt the blood rushing through my eyeballs and a glimmer of yellow was staring back at me through the visor mirror, my sclera now riddled with bulging red veins that I could feel every time I blinked.

"Jax!" Carrie screamed in fear.

Kyle pulled the car over and bailed, Carrie was seconds behind him, and they locked me inside while I writhed in pain. I watched as my teeth sharpened and the throbbing of my gums eventually erupted into fangs four times the size of my regular teeth.

It took enormous amounts of strength, but I was able to hold back any further transformation…at least for now.

Christian peered in through the window carefully and pointed to the sewer gates not too far from us. We had halted just in time.

"There's screams coming from there, stay here, we'll go check it out," He ordered.

I sat as I watched from afar as they walked down into a shallow gully, what looked like an old lake that had long since dried up exposing a huge circular tunnel secured by a large iron gate.

There was a single beam of light coming from within the tunnel and I caught a whiff of something familiar to me. The stench of a hell hound, I could hear the claws scraping against the concrete like a lazy child who didn't pick up their feet when they walked, I could smell the old, dried blood from the last victims.

Kyle was in front of the others with a rifle and as stupid as it looked, Christian had a bright orange super-soaker loaded with colloidal silver. The girls were hanging back about 20ft away from the gate as steam and growling began to echo out.

I leapt from the jeep and bolted down the hill and stood 2 feet taller than usual behind Christian. His eyes locked with mine, this was his first time seeing this side of me, he wasn't afraid though, he was in awe and smiled at me with an excited expression. I could hear the lump in Kyle's throat as he looked up at me and back down as my hands continued to morph into weapons.

The sound inside the tunnel wasn't from one werewolf, there were many, I could hear them as they made their way closer to us and I could hear the sound of a man behind me as he disarmed Celinde by kicking her in the back of the knees. She fell to the ground, and he gripped her tightly by the hair as he stood over her waiting for us to react.

I took five steps forward and he saw my face, he let her go as his jaw flew open.

"There are others?" He mumbled.

"If you know, then you must be one?" Kyle question.

"Maybe I am, Blondie here looks pretty tasty," he snickered.

Christian's face darkened and I exposed my fangs a little more, but he didn't shudder. Christian didn't hesitate and sprayed a stream of colloidal at him, but he didn't flinch, steam or bubble. He merely laughed.

There was a pounding of footsteps behind us, and the gate swung open with three werewolves bounding out.

"Get to the cars!" I yelled.

I lowered my head and darkened my expression as I let the beast inside free. My chest puffed out, my feet shattered my shoes, and my clothes were rags as they fell from my body, I was now complete.

I let out a deep growl, these wolves were far smaller than I was, they seemed to stay away from the human who'd just struck Celinde. The smaller of them launched and threw his whole weight at my body, he sunk his fangs into my arm, but I was able to shake him off, the other two were following the others and I ran after them, Celinde was driving while Christian clung to a ladder prepping the tank with his free hand from the roof as the truck moved, Carrie was driving the jeep and Kyle was up through the sunroof with water guns.

I was larger and faster and managed to leap onto the back of the fire truck before I exerted too much of my energy.

But these smaller wolves were fast and the man with them was following us in an old white van as they sprung along the side of the roads, ripping down trees and turning over cars.

"Get us out of town Celinde!" Christian yelled.

He was right, this would be a bloodbath if we stayed in the city, we had to get them out where it was less populated.

The jeep went first, and we followed closely behind. Christian was careful to keep his distance from me as I stood in a stance ready to pounce if any of them got too close, Christian had the hose ready and was prepared to fire it as our first line of defense.

These wolves were reckless but fortunately for us, I had a size advantage—and we were well prepared.

We'd soon learn if that was going to be enough.

The larger of them was gaining on us and Christian let the hose loose on him, he curled up in pain and let out a loud whimper and he tumbled to the ground, this only angered the other two more, they weren't playing now, they pushed forward in the very moment we cleared the road and I lunged forward ripping one to the ground, Carrie whipped the jeep around and shone the spotlights in our direction while Kyle and Christian did what they could to take down the other one. The white van was minutes behind us, he'd stopped to collect the fallen wolf, the back door was open, and flung the light-colored wolf into a stream of colloidal Kyle had fired.

The wolf from the van emerged, his fur dripping off his body, his face burnt, skin still oozing, every time he healed his body trapped the silver, there was too much of it on him. He pressed forward in my direction preparing to take another shot at me, but he was weak, the man followed behind him with a shotgun in hand, he had it aimed at me.

"Put it down, and this can end here!" Christian commanded.

The wolves were all covered in blood and silver, barely able to peel themselves from the gravel. We had successfully taken them down, but not for long. They would eventually heal.

"I'm just trying to protect my kids," the man cried.

Carrie emerged from the jeep and joined Kyle through the sunroof.

"Your kids?" she echoed his words.

"They don't know what they're doing, I will keep them locked up," he begged.

"You can't contain werewolves, you don't know the damage werewolves can cause," Carrie shouted.

"I know better than you girl, I saw werewolves tear down a ski lift cable on our trip at Hurricane Ridge, I saw my sons maul my wife to death," He cried as he pointed the shotgun to the back of the head of the wolf from the van.

"But he's my son…" he whimpered.

The same wolf turned and lashed out, ripping the gun from the man's hand, growling down at him as the father sunk to the ground in obedience.

"You have no control over them," Kyle growled.

I walked forward and tore the wolf to the ground and let out a howl.

Passers-by in a car stopped, our cars all blocking the road, before they could turn around the younger of the wolves launched for the car, ripped the driver's door off and ripped them out, threw them against the body of the vehicle, and began feasting before us all.

Kyle tried to spray him, but he seemed stronger from feeding, the hunger made them crazed. I pulled the body from him, his fangs gnashing and snapping at me, he leaned further forward as I tried to fight him back, but his fangs had sunk into my neck, I drop to the ground and rolled him over and tore away a chunk of flesh from his sternum with my muzzle, I couldn't stop, the fulfillment of allowing myself to feed on a warm body, was ecstasy. The screams felt more distant, the shock was the only thing I felt, it was eyes upon me as they all watched on in fear.

"Jax!" Christian yelled.

But I wasn't going to listen to anyone. While I fed the man loaded up his sons, took off back to the town, but Kyle and Carrie followed them.

"We can't let them get away!" Carrie yelled to Celinde, and she and Kyle piled into the Jeep.

"We'll stay with Jax," Christian yelled back as they disappeared down the road.

I pulled the wolf apart even more, breaking bones as I went, but I kept him alive. I sat on the road enjoying my meal as my prey watched me in his rare moments of consciousness. I knew it was wrong, but I couldn't stop. I felt stronger, bigger, more powerful, but less controlled, my focus was blurred. Maybe this is how Noah felt, every feed took away another piece of my humanity.

"Stop Jax!" Christian yelled.

I pulled my eyes away from my live beating meal and squared Christian off.

"This isn't you; Lupe wouldn't want this for you," he sighed. He dropped the hose, completely disarming himself, giving in to trust. He trusted me not to kill him.

I stood up and threw the wolf to the side of the road and slowly, painfully forced the beast back inside. That werewolf should be dead, if not now... soon.

Celinde came around from the driver's side with a camping shower bag of water and some of my clothes.

"Help him," she said to Christian.

Christian strung up the shower bag and held the nozzle for me as I stood on the road naked washing the blood and flesh from my body. My skin was covered in red spots from the bristly barbs of hair, my eyes were red and glassy, and my fingernails were bruised and raw.

"I'm sorry," I whispered with a broken voice.

"You don't need to apologize," Christian answered.

"I do, I lost control. That's not the man I want to be," I sighed.

"We need to go and make sure that body isn't coming back to take a bite out of you," Celinde groaned from the driver's seat.

"I'll go," Christian said as he armed himself with a water gun and stepped around the truck. Celinde and I followed as I wrestled pants on.

"It's gone!" Kyle yelled.

"Well, now what?" Celinde sulked.

"We gotta go and find it," I sighed.

"Back to the sewer gate?" Christian asked.

"Yep, that's where he'll take them. That gate had a latch and a lock. He knew what he was doing," Celinde had observed it all closely.

"Pack it up!" I banged on the truck.

Kyle and Carrie were ahead of us and driving into danger.

V.J.Garland

Chapter Five

Celinde

I drove the truck all the way back to town, Christian was frozen, staring out the window, his eyes fixed on the jeep as we finally caught up with them. We turned the corner down to where we first encountered the man and the three other werewolves.

"Are we going in there?" I stammered; fear rattling my voice.

"I don't know, just stay behind me, okay?" he grasped my hand softly and held my gaze.

I nodded my head slowly.

I was afraid, really afraid. There were three of them if the other made his way back, but even two was one more than what we had. Jax was big, unpredictable, and slightly slower because of his size. He liked to think he had everything under control, but I knew better than to be alone with him in his alternate form.

Carrie was the first to leave the jeep, she was brave and wild, so capable of a life on the road gunning down what were meant to be imaginary beings. Kyle was next armed with more colloidal-filled water guns.

Jax emerged from the truck. He looked a hot mess; his face was black and blue and that wasn't the worst of it. His entire body was riddled with red angry lesions, his eyes were bloodshot, you could tell every single blink was a wash of pain and I felt pity for him. It was freezing outside, he wore nothing but torn pants, but he was bigger now than yesterday, his pant button and zipper didn't reach, and his thighs were threatening to burst through his jeans, his shoulders were broader, his chest puffier and his jaw squarer. Whatever the change did to him, it made him considerably larger even as a human.

Christian stared at me a moment longer and twiddled his Mario mustache at me to catch my attention.

"Sorry, I was deep in thought..." I smiled softly.

"If you're afraid, stay here," he urged.

"No, I'm good, let's go!" I perked myself up.

But I wasn't ready for this, I was shitting myself. Every thought and scenario rushed through my thoughts; I was grateful Carrie was able to read my body language so well.

"Snap out of it," She pressed a water gun into my chest.

"Yep, I'm coming," I sighed as I accepted my status as the class pussy.

Christian grabbed my hand and towed me slightly behind him and I willingly clung to him, memorizing every wrinkle of his hand, the warmth he generated, and the kindness of his heart.

We approached the gate and screams of pain and angst could be heard, but only just. They came from deep within the tunnel.

"Okay, are we ready for this?" Jax asked.

"No, but let's do it anyway," Kyle sighed.

I suddenly realized I wasn't the only pussy amongst us, we all hindered some fears and uncertainties about this.

Jax reach out his hand, I could hear the crushing of his bones, his veins popping as they stretched to accommodate his sheer size.

"Does that hurt?" Carrie asked as she watched on.

"Yes," Jax turned to her as his eyes began to glow their yellow hue, tears stained with blood were sucked into the pores on his face.

Christian held me tightly. My head barely escaped the height of his shoulders, and I welcomed his warmth wrapping around me, he silently kissed the top of my head and rested his chin on me as we waited for Jax to strike the cage and unleash hell upon us.

He raised his hand and thrashed it down on the bars. The cage had been locked from the inside this time.

Jax went first, followed by Carrie and Kyle. I turned to face Christian as he loosened his hold on my waist.

"Before we potentially die…Would you go to dinner with me sometime?" I smiled.

He stroked my cheek softly and smiled a big fluffy smile.

"I thought you'd never ask," he nodded cheekily.

His hand held my chin and he leaned down to kiss me.

"You guys…really? After all this time, you chose now?" Carrie groaned as she walked back to the entry.

"Sorry, I might never get the chance again…" I muttered as I headed past her.

"Sorry Care!" Christian smirked as he pressed past her.

She followed behind us and gently closed the gate to disguise that it hadn't been opened.

We walked through what felt like miles of murky water and the smell of rotten vegetation. There were a fair few rats and an undisclosed number of insects.

"We're getting closer," Jax whispered.

The low howls and growls became louder and louder with every step I took, I was walking towards uncertainty, likely death.

Jax began to morph, letting the beast tear through his body and we all stayed a few extra feet back.

We turned a corner and there was the father with an oil lamp in hand just inches from another gate. His eyes were filled with worry. Hands were reaching for him, but he backed away. There was begging, crying, and mauling echoing throughout the tunnels.

"You're feeding them!" Carrie screamed.

Carried pushing him out of the way and began trying to unlock the cage, scrambling over the man for a key.

"Where is the key!" She screamed.

The wolves were feasting, distracted from our presence. Jax was trying to keep his cool, but his fangs were excited and ready to sink into the next body that rubbed him the wrong way.

Carrie's demands were hopeless, he would never tell us. Kyle searched him and shook him, a grunt met Jax at the cage as he faced off the with the same wolf he had almost eaten. His two younger brothers making a feast out of a group of teenage girls, one shaking uncontrollably in the corner.

"There's more than three," I tapped Christian anxiously.

"I know, I counted five, they must have turned others," his face was white.

"We shouldn't be here..." I fidgeted.

Jax began lashing at the gate, his size alone would snap the bars like toothpicks.

He ripped the hinges from the frames, forgetting the rest of us were humans.

The wolves stirred and Jax took a blow to the largest, knocking him into the group of girls.

"Run!" Kyle yelled.

Carrie lunged into the cell and grabbed two girls and followed behind us as we ran through the tunnel desperate to find the exit.

"Wrong way!" Carrie yelled.

But it was too late, we were backed into a fork, and I had no idea which way to go. I had no time to think and no way out.

"There, climb the ladder!" I yelled. The wolves were close behind us and the ladder lead into a thin shaft that would open onto a street.

I forced the young girls up first, Carrie was next.

"I can't get it open," the first yelled as she tried to spin the manhole cover.

"Hurry!" Christian yelled. His water gun was already empty, and mine was rather small, better for close range.

Kyle threw Christian his spare.

It kept them back but only for seconds, Jax was nowhere to be seen until a flame from the lantern lit up a cloud of fumes from the methane.

Christian turned to me. "Get out of here, try that one!" He ordered as he pointed behind the wolves.

"I'll cover you…go!" he ordered.

I did as he said and leapt over and around the wolves as he sprayed them with colloidal disabling them for short seconds as they writhed in pain as the silver melted through their flesh.

"I'm out," Kyle announced to Christian loud enough for me to hear.

Jax was ripping through them, but it wasn't enough, they healed just as fast and began to fight back.

"Turn me!" Christian yelled.

My stomach sunk as I forced the manhole open, the first of the teens were out only a few meters down the road in a suburban street.

I heard Jax's deep growl and Christian cry out in pain as his knees met the ground with a powerful thud. I climbed back down the shaft and watched as Christian exploded into a beast of an almost comparable size to Jax.

"Nooo!" I cried. Kyle raced up the shaft as he forced me back onto the street. The others were out now, and Carrie rushed to my side.

The massacre below us was loud and woke the street of residents, lights began to flicker on, and ladies came out in their dressing gowns. A blast echoed and the road began to shake as some sections started to crumble into the earth in places where the tunnel gave way. I heard the howling of smaller wolves, and the smell of singed hair enveloped the space around me.

"Christian!" I yelled down the shaft.

"Cel, I don't think they made it, nobody could survive that blast," Carrie sighed.

Kyle rushed back down the shaft even though it choked him with the smoke, the heat of the handles was enough to burn his hands, but he pressed on and dropped to the bottom.

"What do you see?" Carrie yelled out.

He didn't reply, but I heard more than one voice, I felt relief that it was a voice—not a growl.

Jax's head emerged first from the tunnel and Carrie strangled him with a hug before he could peel himself out.

"The others?" I asked.

"Christian's okay," he smiled.

"Those others are dead?" Carrie asked.

"They should be, they took the impact of that blast," he explained.

Kyle appeared next holding Christian up as best he could, he was weak and barely conscious.

Jax sat in the road naked, an older lady rushed out to bring him her robe.

"We gotta get out of here," Kyle said to Carrie as I tried to help with Christian. Kyle took off his jacket and wrapped it around Christian's waist.

Jax's ears twitched, and Christian's eyes glowed a shade of yellow as his head sat in my lap.

"Get these people off the street...Now!" Jax ordered.

"What is it?" Kyle asked.

"There are some still alive, still down there..." Jax answered.

"You! get these girls to a hospital!" Carrie shouted to a middle-aged couple gawking from their patio.

One girl had a significant gash across her cheek, the other a large bite mark that looked old and infected on her forearm. They must have been down there for days; they were dirty and afraid.

"Everyone off the street!" Kyle was in his zone, policing the neighborhood, even if it wasn't his jurisdiction.

The earth below us rattled, the heat was emitting into the pavement and began to steam, the soles of our shoes felt hot, and then there was more crackling and rumbling.

In the corner of my eye, I spied the father of the wolves escaping from another manhole just off the street we were on.

Before I could yell to the others, the werewolves we presumed dead for only minutes exploded through the manholes, ripping them wide open. They were in bad shape, some with fur and blood dripping, the silver of the colloidal danced in their veins beneath the moonlight adding luminescence to them, others still had embers of fire racing through their fur singeing them bald. Healing set in quickly for those only suffering from the fire. The others with colloidal were scratching their skin open desperate for the silver to leave their bodies.

"We need to go!" I shouted to Jax.

But he was already back in his larger fiercer form ready to pounce, he stood over the rest of us guardingly. Like a mastiff to its owner.

The humans on the street fled for their homes and cars and werewolves the size of teenagers sprung after them. Kyle and Christian worked together, Christian's eyes glowed yellow and his fangs were stained with his own blood as he tore one to the ground.

"We need to get the truck!" Carrie grasped my hand ready to speed off on foot.

"Alone?" I shuddered.

"Now! Before anyone notices we are gone," I agreed with a nod and leapt to my feet.

We sprinted hard and fast down the streets to the lights that illuminated the park.

"I'll get on the hose, you drive," Carrie ordered.

I rolled up the windows, I knew that wouldn't protect me, but it was something. Carrie was pulling on the gear as she sat atop the tank and clung for dear life whilst I raced back through the streets. In the headlights I could see Christian on the ground, he was outnumbered.

"Spray!" I yelled, but Carrie was already on it. She blew away the two smaller werewolves while Jax took on the remaining, Kyle was locked in a garage with some of the residents, but the youngest of the wolves was thrashing and sniffing about at the door, I could only see the tops of heads through the plastic windows at the top of the roller door.

"Get me closer!" Carrie yelled.

Christian heard us and raced for the garage door grabbing the wolf and rolling down the driveway in a pile of dust.

"Move Christian!" Carrie shouted, but she didn't hold back a second longer.

Christian bounded for the front of the truck and locked eyes with me just for a second if only to let me know he was okay. He sprung for Jax and did what he could to put them down or at least chase them off for now.

Carrie freed the garage full of people and leapt down from the truck with the hose, I just took orders for where I needed to drive. She passed me the last water gun through the window just before going to collect Kyle, Christian and Jax they turned back to their human forms. The other werewolves weren't dead, but they were defeated and unable to move, they had been so heavily soaked in colloidal.

"Now what?" Kyle asked.

"We take them with us…" Christian sighed.

"Just kill them!" Carrie screamed.

"We've been trying! they keep coming back," Jax explained.

"Noah's dead…there's got to be some way!" Christian growled.

"There is, we hold them until we figure it out," Jax sighed.

"Hold them? Where do you want to hold them exactly, Jax?" Christian raged.

"Everyone just think! for a moment," Jax was equally frustrated but had the sense to control himself. I worried that Christian didn't have the same measure of control.

I walked over to Christian and handed him a pair of his pants.

"That's twice tonight I've seen you naked..." I tried to joke, but I immediately felt regret as I quickly realized this wasn't the time or place to be cracking seedy flirts.

He just looked down at me, took the pants, and pulled them on never tearing his gaze away.

Carrie felt the ominous doubt trickling through my spine and darted a look of care and love my way. She knew I wasn't the flirt; I wasn't someone who said things like this, so it didn't come naturally at all which made the embarrassment all the more heavy.

Christian moved toward me ignoring Kyle and Jax's discussion in the background. Jax was sitting on top of the eldest and Kyle had two guns pointed at the others, but they were still too weak to move.

"Sorry..." I sighed as I shifted my eyes away from Christian's.

His hand reached for mine, and he gently kissed me on the head.

"It's been a long night…" he grunted. His eyes still had lingering flecks of yellow in them, his hands slightly bigger than before, cuticles red with dried blood.

"It'll be daylight soon, let's tie these guys up and move them to Wapato. It's abandoned, it'll be safe for a short while," Kyle ordered.

Christian left my side and raced to the triple searching for ropes, anything to bind them.

"Are you okay?" Carrie came over and quizzed me as best friends do.

"I don't know why I said that…" I sighed.

"I'm so embarrassed Care," She hugged me tightly and brought me to the opposite side of the triple so the others wouldn't see us.

"He's unsure of himself and probably about what his change means for you guys, don't be so hard on yourself," as rough and tough as Carrie was, she was great at logical thinking.

"You also need to think about what that whole transformation means for you! Don't just be okay with it because you liked him yesterday, today he is a different person," She added with wisdom.

"How do you date a werewolf? What the fuck am I even saying…" I shrugged.

"Maybe just start back at the beginning and figure out if you like this new person as much as you like the old one, it's okay if you don't," she assured me.

"Can you guys go get the Jeep," Jax looked between me and Christian.

"Sure," I nodded.

Christian opened the door for me and helped me up into the truck. He started the ignition and set off down the road to the park.

"How are you feeling?" I asked.

"Different, I can't explain it," he sighed.

"Thank you…" I tried to catch his stare.

"For what?" he asked.

"If you hadn't of done what you did, we wouldn't have gotten out alive," I sighed

He nodded and tossed me the keys to the Jeep.

"Meet you back there…" he said through a forced smile.

He waited for me to start the jeep and made sure I went ahead of him. He was different, he was cold and numb. Lupe's letters described this in all the pages she wrote about Noah. If I pursued Christian, would I be doomed to the same fate as her? I had questions and nobody around me could answer them.

We weaved through the streets back to the scene of decimation, I was careful not to move over unstable ground.

There were ambulances rolling onto the scene and police sirens not far behind us.

"Move!" Kyle ordered.

The guys shuffled the young men into the vehicles, and they weren't gentle about it.

"I'll stay in here with them, make sure they don't get loose," Jax nodded to Kyle.

"You're the boss!" Kyle closed the doors to the boot of the jeep.

"How far away is this place?" Carrie asked Kyle.

"20 minutes," He replied.

"You drive," He tossed her the keys.

"Come on," Christian pulled my hand and walked us off to the truck.

"Let's roll!" Christian shouted through the window.

As we left the street in a thousand pieces of rubble and sprinkled in unintelligible questions that no sane human could answer, we passed the police entering.

"Well good thing we are in a fire truck!" Christian snickered.

"Those people are going to have to be evacuated, Christian! The entire neighborhood is at risk of going up in flames all because we went chasing after monsters in the night," I growled.

"Monsters…" he sighed.

"I didn't mean you, I just meant we didn't think any of this through,"

"It's fine, Celinde. I understand," he huffed.

I was making a mess of my words tonight, every one of them directed at Christian. I was anxious, nervous, and suddenly all my feelings of giddiness and teenage-like angst became fear over my loss of control.

V.J.Garland

Chapter Six

Christian

She had no idea that every single feeling I had was to fuel a hunger that had never been fed. I'd never felt anything like it, it wasn't like alcoholism or drugs it was something completely different, it was like oxygen and being told I couldn't have it—even though I needed it to survive.

We finally rolled up to the prison and I tore at the gates with Jax to open them.

"This place is being watched…" Carrie yelled as she pointed to security cameras as they glazed over the grounds on timers.

"Now what?" Kyle asked as he turned and stopped.

"Lethal dose and toss them over the fence," Carrie suggested.

"We're actually running low. The tank is almost empty," I sighed.

"Fuck…" Kyle grumbled.

"The eldest, he's got to be their leader… kill him!" Kyle growled.

I went to the jeep and dragged him out and onto the ground and he was ready to submit. He couldn't have been any older than 21. Just a kid who went skiing at the exact wrong time.

"Can you control yourself?" I shoved him into Jax.

"No, I can't," he sighed.

His eyes glowed orange and the colloidal could be seen fluttering in his bloodshot veins each time he blinked.

"Can you try?" Jax groaned.

"Why should I?" He sighed with defeat.

"Because if you don't, we'll have to kill you," I explained.

"If you can give me your word you'll try, you can join us, I'll help you," Jax sighed.

Carrie gasped as Celinde gripped her arm and dropped to the floor.

"Jax!" Kyle snapped.

"This isn't the life for you, Kyle," Jax snapped.

"Wait… what the fuck is going on?" Celinde screamed.

I didn't like what was happening, but I knew what Jax was doing was to protect those of us who were still human. Because this life had taken everything from us with a split-second decision.

Suddenly, I wasn't a firefighter, or some guy chasing a beautiful woman hoping she'd share a smile with me at all the right moments. I was a monster, and I would just as quickly snatch away her life in a fit of rage if she upset me.

"Then turn me, Jax! cause I'm in this with you for life!" Kyle yelled.

"You need to be you! You need to get the girls out of here…" I pressed him against the truck before Jax could.

"Go!" I sighed.

"Christian!" Celinde was trying her hardest to pull me away from him.

I barely felt her punching me as Carrie dragged her back and Kyle pushed me off of him.

"Christian!" Celinde cried.

I walked over to her as Carrie and Kyle pulled her into the car.

"I'm sorry," I sighed as I pressed my hand against her window.

Her face was wet, pale, and cold. Like a child who'd had to return a lost puppy to its original owners.

"In another life, we had a chance," I sobbed.

"You! You did this!" She screamed through the window at Jax. His head was lowered as he avoided her despair.

Carrie cried as she held Celinde, and Kyle drove them away from the prison as fast as he could go.

"I hope you know what you're doing!" I yelled at Jax.

"I'm protecting them, something you can't do right now. I can smell your desire to feed on her, don't deny it," Jax snapped.

"I had it under control," I sighed.

"For how long, Christian?" he asked.

"For her... forever," I sighed.

"You're wrong! Noah tortured and taunted Lupe for five years! Do you want to repeat his mistakes, or do you think maybe that girl deserves to live a full life without terrors going bump in the night? I saw what that did to Lupina, do you know what she looked like when I met her? She was lifeless, she was skin and bones and so malnourished she couldn't feel the cold on the tips of her fingers. You don't get to decide that fate for Celinde!" Jax took a breath and sat on the dirt road.

I finally understood him, I understood why he was so strong and in control.

"He's right, you can't stop it," The oldest sighed.

"What's your name kid?" I asked.

"Seb," he replied.

"You've been feeding this whole time?" Jax asked.

Seb broke into tears as he nodded through his weeping.

"We fed on our mother, we killed her..." his heart was broken and for the first time, I saw him as a human being instead of an animal that needed to be put down.

"Do you know who turned you?" Jax asked.

"A werewolf with bulging orange eyes and a balding muzzle. There were others with him, they didn't all get along, they were fighting, trying to kill each other," he explained.

"Noah's rival, he's the one who killed my brother," Jax sighed.

"Our dad, Wesley tried to protect us, googled everything to fix us but we couldn't contain it, so he chained us up in the sewers," Seb explained.

"And he brought you snacks..." I glowered.

"Look man, nobody was thinking, this is the longest I've been human in weeks, I wish I'd died in that field..." He sobbed some more.

"You seem to be having a pretty good time out there," I snapped.

"Easy for you to say when you're new, taunt me again when you've tasted your first drop of blood or felt a warm body in your mouth still pulsating. Now imagine that's your girl..." he challenged me.

"I would never do that to her..." I growled.

"And I would never kill my own mother... but she was delicious!" his eyes stared at me hard.

"Seb!" shouted one of his brothers.

"That's Mike and Tristan," he introduced reluctantly.

The youngest, Mike was crying, he was no older than 15, Tristan looked to be around 19.

"You're just a little kid..." Jax sighed as he went to sit beside Mike.

"That's enough for now," I forcefully closed the conversation.

"We'll help you stay human, but you have to try and not kill anyone," Jax looked between the boys.

"There were other werewolves who got away," Tristan sighed.

"We'll find them, Jax nodded.

My phone rang in my pocket, and I moved away from the others to answer it.

"Just give me dinner, you owe me that. Then I'll disappear and forget everything..." it was Celinde.

"Wolf Tree Brewery in Newport, 5 pm," I hung up the phone before anyone could say anything.

"I hope you know what you're doing..." Jax growled.

We crammed into the triple and made our way towards Newport; the drive was only 2 hours and somewhere on this road I knew Celinde was making the same journey. There's no way I should be feeling all the things I felt for her, maybe it was the werewolf in me heightening my emotions, but she deserved more than what she got.

"Here, before you go and make any stupid decisions, remind yourself why we are here," Jax punch me in the chest with Lupe's diary as I jumped out of the truck.

I nodded as he waved me off.

I was early and Jax and the others had dropped me off on the banks at Idaho Point where there was no traffic or persons to come across me. I sat there staring at the water for hours reading and thinking.

So treacherous she was—the water. Calm and beautiful on top but under her layers she would rip you down with a current, and hold you there till all life escaped you, all memories washed away and all that would remain to be found was a vessel. I felt like I was the ocean, I would suck Celinde into my chaos and either kill her or chip away at her until she had nothing left to give.

I walked hesitantly towards the brewery, she was sitting there with Carrie and Kyle with pints of beers.

Kyle and Carrie nodded to me as they got up to leave, Celinde didn't look up, but she knew I was there. I sat down in front of her and reached out and held her hand.

"I didn't know he was going to do that, I'm sorry," I sighed.

"But you didn't fight him on it, Christian!" she met my gaze.

"What kind of life can I offer you when I am this…it makes sense," I shrugged.

"We never even got a chance to try, how do you know it can't work?" she sighed.

I placed Lupe's diary on the table between us and I felt her heart sink.

"This… this is no life for anyone, I can't do to you what Noah did to Lupina," I gasped.

"Lupe chose to stay!" Celinde argued.

"Lupe was an idiot! I'm sorry, but she got herself killed. She was kind, too kind, and she loved Noah so hard it killed her, Celinde. I can't repeat their past, that's not why I joined this fucking circus," I confessed.

"Then we change the outcome, there's got to be a way!" She pressed.

"There is… you forget you ever met me, let me be a ghost in your past," I sighed.

"All I have to give you now is a life on the run," I added as I shook my head.

"Fine, but you owe me tonight, one night…" she sighed.

"One dinner…" I corrected her.

"If that's all I get, I get a whole night…" she sobbed.

"I want to know everything there is to know about you, and then I'll walk away, I promise," she added.

"Why open yourself up for heartache like this?" I asked.

"Because there have been men my whole life, but not a single one like you, nobody ever taught me how to drive a fire truck or shoot werewolves off of a moving vehicle… Nobody ever threw away their life to make sure I got to live mine," her eyes were dark with tears.

"Are we romanticizing sacrifices now?" I chuckled.

"I guess we are…" she smiled.

"Let's get some food to go?" I asked.

"Yeah, think I could use a walk," she nodded.

We collected a bag of fries and burgers and made our way back to the bay where Jax had dropped me off.

"So those other werewolves? what's their story?" she asked.

"Once we got it out of them, it was rather terrible, I think I understand their grief.

"The youngest is only 15 I think," I added.

"That's going to be a hard transition," she sighed.

"He's young, we'll work on it together," I replied.

"I believe in you," she smiled.

"Where will you go?" I asked.

"I have some family in Salem, I'll stay there while I figure it out," she explained.

"You?" She asked.

"Jax wants to hunt down those other werewolves, I don't really think he's thinking straight, his mind is muddled," I confessed

"That's what humanizes him, Christian. Jax is a good man because he sees the good in others. I don't know a lot of people with a heart that big," She sighed.

"That big heart is going to get us all killed," I muttered.

"You don't trust the others?" I asked.

"Why would I? They are virtually unkillable, what does that mean for me and Jax? Are we the same or can we be taken out by them if we don't sleep with one eye open?" I quizzed.

We sat by the bank and the breeze whipped through her long hair as I unpacked our food.

We sat back-to-back leaning on one another while we ate our food. I felt sickly eating it, it wasn't quenching anything or filling my pockets of hunger, but I forced it down regardless, I was desperate to give her the last human moments I had to offer.

"If anyone can get through this and find peace after it's you guys. Kyle is a little pissed," she laughed.

I snickered at her remark.

"Tell him I'm sorry I took his spot, for what it's worth we don't see eye to eye on this," I sighed.

She turned to face me and stared for a moment trying to memorize my face for her memory bank the way she held my hand in that tunnel.

"I wish we got a better ending, don't think I didn't want to date you," I smiled as I held her face in my hands.

"Hell, I saw a future with you, werewolf hunting aside, you were why I came along for this ride. You walked into my fire station, and I wanted you, I needed you and I was prepared to kill monsters beside you," a bloodied tears welled in my eyes.

"And now…" she asked.

"And now, I'm the monster," I professed.

She climbed on top of me and let her passion loose on my lips as I guided her thighs down over and around my own.

She had this incredible warmth about her, a warmth that made you feel like you were home, safe, and loved.

"I can't imagine my world with you gone..." she whimpered into my mouth.

"I've only known you a little over a week, and somehow I'll never be the same," I whispered back.

She pulled my shirt up and over my head and I unbuttoned her blouse, as she unbuttoned her jeans. If we only had tonight, we'd take all of it without regret or shame. I'd feel every ounce of her body against mine and I'd hold onto that as tight as my humanity for as long as I could. I knew once I was gone, I might not find my way back to her.

We sat in the dark for hours, making love and learning about one another, all to be forgotten tomorrow.

It was past 2 am when Jax rolled around in the truck with Seb, Tristan, and Mike.

"Sorry guys, but it's time," Jax's expression was sad and broken. He had known heartbreak once before himself.

"Can we drop you somewhere Celinde?" he asked.

She nodded as she climbed into the back of the truck and sat close to me holding onto my warmth.

"South Beach RV Park," she mumbled.

I wrapped my arms around her and stroked her hair as we turned into the bay where Carrie and Kyle waited by a bonfire. We all climbed out of the truck.

"So, we get a proper goodbye?" Carrie grabbed Jax and hugged him.

"It was too risky back there before I knew what I know now. Here, take this," He held out a wad of cash for Carrie.

"No!" she laughed nonsensically.

"Nonsense, I have a fallback, you don't. Take it," he pressed the money into her hands.

"Thanks for looking out for me! I'll miss you," she smiled.

"You're really gonna make me babysit the girls..." Kyle grumbled.

"There's nobody else I trust more," Jax smiled as he pulled Kyle into a bear hug.

"Take care of yourself!" Kyle smacked him on the back gently.

"Celinde, I'm sorry... I dragged you into this and now I feel like I'm taking away your future," he sighed.

She moved away from me and went to hug Jax.

"Just look after him, and when you've done whatever, it is you need to do, bring him back," she sighed.

But there was no coming back, and everyone knew it. It was common knowledge just from the glance we shared, this would claim our lives like it did Noah.

"I'll do what I can," he patted her hair.

"We should go..." Jax whispered to me as I held Celinde for the last time.

"Take care of him," Celinde growled to Jax.

"All of you take care of each other!" Jax pointed more specifically to Kyle followed by a wink.

"Don't say goodbye..." she sighed as I held my lips on her forehead.

"I'll see you in my dreams," I smiled as I pulled away from her, held her hands and kissed them one final time before using my superhuman speed to rush myself into the truck before I could regret it.

Jax wasn't far behind and was quick to remove us from the situation. Seb was awake in a passenger seat and his brothers were asleep in the back.

"How're you doing there Seb?" I asked trying to glaze over our first interactions.

"That silver stuff is still kicking my ass if that's what you wanna know…" he shrugged.

"Maybe that's what is keeping you human?" Jax questioned.

"It doesn't burn so much in my human form, but when I'm a werewolf, it's like acid," he explained.

"I know, I've felt it before," Jax nodded as he recalled the pain.

"Keep that stuff away from me…" I laughed.

"Get some sleep Christian," Jax ordered as I climbed into the cab.

Chapter Seven

Jax

The more of us there were, the harder it would be to control everyone, and I was barely holding it together myself. I had more restraint than the others, but how long could I keep up the charade.

I was hungry—hunger that couldn't be quenched by a cheeseburger and fries or a flight to Philadelphia for a cheesesteak, what I craved was right under my nose every time I turned a corner on a street, it was raw beating and breathing.

Disorder didn't take long to arrive in our camp, and I began to see where it all unraveled so quickly for Noah and his lesser wolves. It was hard enough keeping myself in check and now I had a horny firefighter and three teenagers who had been well acquainted with the taste of a live feed.

When you're this powerful, why should you listen to what anyone else has to say? I just hoped Christian had the strength to stop himself from turning back and could keep his focus on what we had set out to do… to avenge Noah and Lupe and put an end to all the werewolves he had created.

Warrenton must have been overrun, I could sense an overwhelming scent of blood and despair in the air going north, it was coming from Warrenton and news reports backed that up. The other wolves would be drawn there by the smell. I had hoped to leave and never return—that all the trouble would follow me, but it didn't, it was right where I left it, at home. We drove through the night until we reached the town, it was a shambles, buildings burnt to the foundations, rubble-strewn, and blood splatter-covered abandoned cars, the odd low growl of a werewolf on edge at the invasion of our unfamiliar scent.

"This is the time to unleash and kill any werewolf who isn't one of us, don't hurt any civilians, if there are any left," I ordered.

Seb had steam billowing from his nostrils as they flared through his transformation, the colloidal still dancing in his skin as he fought through the pain, Tristan and Mike weren't far behind, they were starving and desperate to revisit their former bodies, I couldn't smell any humans and deemed it safe to allow them to run.

"And you?" Christian asked looking me up and down.

"I prefer the element of surprise," I smiled as I flared my hands and stretched my jaw just enough to show my claws and fangs.

"So how do we do this?" he asked.

"Kill or try to kill until we find the leader. Kill the leader, kill the pack," I hummed.

"It's weird you know…you had Seb in death's grip and the others weren't going down," Christian questioned.

"He wasn't the pack leader," I sighed.

"Then who?"

"I don't know…" I replied as I sat on a pile of rubble watching the three brothers comb the streets and bound from street signs to traffic lights, and off of old police vehicles and trucks.

Warrenton had come to an immediate halt. There were signs of failed defense and then certain defeat. It had become a ghost town, no cars were coming in or going out, it was just forgotten…gone from the world and deserted to the monsters.

Daylight was fading and the streetlights flickered, no longer able to hold their strong consistent beams.

Seb emerged from a building with a deer in his grasp as he dragged it along the road to where we sat, Mike and Tristan followed with smaller animals more fitting to their own size. Seb dropped the deer in front of Christian and me offering it to share.

"I'm pretty hungry…" Christian sighed.

"First time?" Seb asked as he morphed back.

"Yep," He gulped.

"It's not that bad, there's better, but this helps with those cravings," Seb nodded.

Christian tore off a back hind leg and I took the other while Seb mauled the rest, he had no etiquette left, he was mauling viciously at it, greedily, afraid someone would tear it away from him. Christian forced out his fangs once more and sunk them into the leg with ease.

"Go easy Seb," I joked.

He pulled away from the body and glared up at me.

"We suffered weeks of being starved in those cages…" he gulped.

"It felt like years!" Tristan added.

"I still feel like I'm playing catch up with my hunger," Seb admitted.

"I always feel like that, nothing fills me up," Christian added.

"It's a constant battle," I sighed.

Everyone put their heads back down and forced gulp after gulp down their throats, I was slower to eat than the others. The idea of this made me feel like I would be accepting defeat and accepting this as my ultimate fate… my doom. I wasn't ready to give up, not until I'd cleared out this werewolf infestation.

I got up and wandered the streets, staring into the empty stores where I once sat and drank coffee with Joel, where we shopped for groceries, and he'd fill the cart recklessly just because he knew I was always paying.

Grief has layers, and some of those layers were so thin that at times the sadness tore through them, but most of the layers were thick, malleable, and allowed me to be sad without it completely shredding me to pieces.

But most days I forced it to the deepest darkest parts of my soul so I could deal with it later, I wasn't ready to grieve, not the way one should.

I heard footsteps behind me, Christian's. And the outpouring of questions was building on his lips as he reluctantly opened pandora's box with one sentence.

"Where did it happen?" he asked.

"Down at cannon beach, it's not too far from here," I answered with a sad grit in my voice.

"Would you go with me?" he asked as he reached into a store for a dead bunch of flowers.

"Sure," I said hesitantly.

"Time for a ride, kids," Christian announced to the others by shouting down the street.

"Shouting?" I hummed.

"If there are others here, they know we are in their territory, it's only a matter of time," Christian exclaimed.

"Are you ready for that?" I asked.

"No," he admitted.

"But I can't live in fear forever, at some point we learn to live with this, or we die," he sighed.

"I don't know how to live like this forever Christian, I don't intend for this to be my forever," I sighed.

"You plan on dying?" he asked as we drove down to Cannon Beach.

"I took an oath when I became a doctor, to serve humanity, to alleviate pain and suffering. Not cause it, I will honor that pledge till the day I die," I replied.

"I took an oath also. *I am bound to protect those who are in danger, those in times of need, those who I would serve,*" Christian sighed.

"Then we ride this out together as long as we can," I nodded as we pulled up at the beach.

I climbed out of the truck and basked in the cold breeze and sea spray as I let my toes feel the sand as I walked out down to the water.

It was peaceful here, so much more peaceful than the last time I had been here. There were no signs of any past disarray, no blood stains, just sand, rocks, and waves crashing as the moon rose into the sky ever so slowly.

"Here," Christian pressed a warm beer into my arm.

"To Noah and Lupe," he sighed.

"To them, and us. May we accomplish all the things we set out to achieve," I took a swig of the beer.

I slumped down into the sand and sat there rolling up my pant legs digging my feet into the wet cold sand like a little kid.

"How do we beat this Jax?" Christian questioned.

"We protect them, from their selves, and us," I said as I watched the others run up and down the beach as they absorbed the freedom.

"We need to figure out what that looks like," he pressed.

"A town, far away from anywhere or anyone. Somewhere we can be free to be who we are without the fear of hurting humans, that is rich with wildlife and preferably not too hot!" I laughed.

"Canada, there's barren land for hundreds of miles, but it's still close enough to civilization if we did need anything. That's where we should build a home," Christian said as he browsed google maps on his phone.

"That's a long way away, you sure?" I asked.

"The further away we are, the better off everyone here will be," he sighed as he removed notifications of missed calls from Celinde.

"Why don't you just block her number?" I asked.

"Because she doesn't deserve that…" he sighed.

"Might be important?" I asked.

"If it was, wouldn't Kyle call you?" he pressed.

"Fair point! You shouldn't have fucked her, now she wants more," I teased.

"What was I meant to do," he sulked.

"Not pity fuck her, terrible idea!" I laughed.

"It wasn't pity, I like her, this whole thing came at the worst time," he slumped back into the sand.

"The whole reason you two met is because of all this werewolf business, it just wasn't meant to be," I sighed.

Seb, Mike, and Tristan came and sat down with us, I handed Seb my beer.

"Can I have some?" Tristan asked.

"Aren't you a bit young?" Christian asked.

"So, I can morph into a killer animal, but I can't have a sip of beer? Touché," he snickered as he took the beer and slugged it back anyway.

"Fair argument I say," I laughed at Christian who seemed amused at Tristan warming to him.

"Why couldn't we all just get along like this at the beginning instead of trying to kill each other?" Christian asked.

"Because you guys were driving around with our main food source, hangry werewolves and humans are a big no-no," Mike the youngest smiled.

"I guess you want some beer too?" I smiled.

He nodded cheerfully as I passed him my bottle.

"What's going to happen if there are others in the town?" Seb asked.

"We kill them if they are uncontrollable, or we adopt them. As we did with you boys," Christian answered.

"Adopt, then what?" Seb asked.

"We build a town… A Werewolf town which will be far away from here, we'll be free to do what we like," I smiled.

"Where?" Tristan probed.

"Probably Yukon," Christian replied.

"Yukon is empty…" he sighed.

"Exactly, we'll be free to swim in every lake or climb every mountain in any form, wolf or naked! You can even bring a fishing pole," I smiled trying to liven up the idea for them.

"We won't be able to hurt anyone?" Mike said with sad eyes.

"Not unless they come looking for us," I sighed as I rested my arm around his shoulders. He leaned into me for a hug he desperately needed. Something so small as a hug, made the world of difference between wolf and man.

"I'm sorry for what's become of your family," I whispered as silent tears dripped down his cheeks, Seb came and sat on his other side offering a more familiar comfort.

"We'll make our own family," Christian announced with enthusiasm.

"What about chicks?" Tristan questioned.

"If you're lucky maybe there's already some werewolf chicks in town," Christian pondered loudly.

"I've never seen a female werewolf, and Lupe had an encounter which could have turned her...it didn't. Maybe it's just males?" I sighed.

"Guess we'll just have to wait and see," Tristan sighed.

"Okay, cheer up boys! The first one to the top of the Haystack, gets to drive the truck back to town," I smiled.

"Which one?" Seb asked.

"The biggest one," I smiled.

The growls were loud but not quite louder than the waves, it was enchanting against the golden hour that drew in closer. I watched on as Christian and the others transformed first, all that blood hit more romantically against the sun, it wasn't so violent, it was magic, we were magic. Not ducks turning into swan's kind of magic, but it was spellbinding non the less.

It was my turn, this was my glory moment, the time I got to enjoy this wild new ride I'd call life, it wasn't meant for me, but I was ready to embrace the complexity it would bring me, the feeling of my knuckles shattering into oblivion every time I forced out the beast, my fangs ripping through my gums, the euphoric feeling of them healing almost immediately as they had sprung back together. There were some lousy lows, but epic highs.

I looked to the others and we lined up alongside one another, Mike the smallest in the front, then Tristan, Seb, Christian, and finally me.

We sprung into the sand, our large paws leaving alarmingly large prints to be swallowed by the surge of waves coming in for the high tide. We all took separate angles, Seb made it first, he was leaner without so much weight to him unlike Christian and me. Mike and Tristan struggled with a lack of coordination and size and worked together to reach the top while I took my time behind them.

The waves were louder from way up here, the water was rising, and we drank in the sunset as it turned from gold to pink, to purple, and finally darkness. The moon glowed over the water and lights from the homes behind us began to like up, twinkling ever so softly behind the truck.

"Do you hear that?" Christian asked as he turned back to his human form.

I nodded and turned my head sharply. Seb was snarling and snapping his jaw as his snout went crazy at a familiar scent wafting towards us.

Mike and Tristan were scurrying to climb down, pouncing from rock to rock and finally swimming the rest of the way back to the shore. The rest of us followed and shook off the water as best we could.

The smell continued to float down from the walkway and in the darkness, two sets of orange eyes could be seen, between them stood the boy's father, Wesley. He had these werewolves beside him on chains with inverted spiked muzzles that would reverse close, similar to a bear trap ripping their heads wide open.

"Dad?" Tristan cried as he dropped to the ground in his human form still depleted from the transformation.

"Come on boys!" He ordered as he gazed between Mike and Seb.

"You can go, I'm staying with Jax," Tristan announced.

"Tristan ?" his dad called with disappointment.

"I won't go back to the sewers and cages! I'm staying with Christian and Jax," he shouted.

"We're a family, we stick together!" He growled back.

"We stopped being a family a long time ago," Mike argued.

"Fine…" he grunted as he loosened his grip on the chains.

"What are you doing!?" Tristan yelled as he ran to hide behind Seb.

He was still very much a scared kid; he had a unique ability, but that never took the fear away from him. He felt vulnerable just like the rest of us.

It had become very clear that their father had long since lost his mind, he was using werewolves to guard himself and to sniff us out after he escaped Portland.

He walked towards me as I turned back into a human, his gaze hard and crazed.

"You'll give me my sons back!" he scowled.

"It's up to them, but if they start killing again you know what will happen," I warned.

"Is that a threat?" he jabbed.

"It's whatever you want it to be," I replied.

Christian was stalking behind me— ready to pounce.

Seb was cautious and had an uneasy look on his face.

"If you don't come with me, there will be bodies strewn on this beach by morning," he yelled.

"What power do you have to say such a thing?" I scowled.

"I can release these beasts in a split second, and they've been starved, ready for the fight," he cackled.

"That's what you do though, isn't it father?" Tristan yelled.

"You starved us and caged us like animals, then used us for your own gain, you didn't give a fuck about mom dying!" Blood began to trickle down his fangs as the rage burned inside him.

"She was a dead weight," he sneered.

"And that's why you let us maul her to death…" Tristan cried as he let out a painful growl.

"Better her than me!" he muttered.

"You're a coward," I growled.

"I survive…" he said in a dark low tone.

Everyone on the beach was turned except for me. The boys had made their choice and chosen to stand with Christian and me…for now.

Their father stood there with wickedness glinting in his eyes from the moonlight, his wolves up on their hind legs and ready to attack. Dark shadows with more orange eyes crowding in behind him.

There must have been about six of them, keeping their distance but it was easy to hear them lashing their tongues licking their snouts as they tore through the beachfront houses, screams ensued as rooftops exploded with more werewolves.

"Get back on the stack, we'll have a clearer view," I ordered.

"We'll be trapped," Tristan was afraid.

"We'll have a better shot up there than down here exposed," I patted him gently on the shoulder before rushing him off back to the rocks.

Wesley stood there fearless as he drank in the anarchy and mayhem, humans evacuated onto the beach and several rushed for the haystack, swimming through the high tide desperate to reach the rocks, wolves on their tails. Tristan did his best to help me as I helped them up, but the stack was steep and slippery from the rain and moss.

I didn't know how long we'd last up here, but I knew I couldn't die on the same beach as Lupe and Joel. I raced down and jumped into the water and paddled my way back to the beach and fought off as many wolves as I could while the humans climbed up the steep rocks.

Hunger set in, laced with aggression and I began ripping through limbs, jaws, anything that entered my grip. I was far bigger than all of them. Christian and Seb jumped down and helped me fight off what we could, but we were vastly outnumbered.

The water was stained crimson, the marine life became abundant and excitable as they feasted on the remains of werewolves and humans alike. The only way we were able to completely put them down was by tearing them completely apart. But more charged us and Seb was down and injured, his excelled healing not enough to help us.

Humans were screaming from the rocks as some fell from the lack of space.

"There's too many of them," I looked to Christian with despair.

He was glaring at the father, he stood there so still, so protected and we began to move in on him, he immediately released his wolves on us, and they were rampant, vicious, and gnarly, more so than the ones that had come down from Warrenton. I took one and Christian the other, but their starvation drove them.

They were harder to take down than the others, I was covered in gashes as soon as my old gashes were healed and had several chunks bitten from me. Christian was often howling in pain. There was an absence of sound as we fought, the other wolves were watching on, Seb had his father under his watch and a paw full of claws holding him by the throat.

Chapter Eight

Celinde

I wasn't ready to go home or see the carnage that I knew awaited. It had been all over the news and in the papers. Something had wiped out the towns and people occupying the top coastal section of Oregon. And I knew exactly what, but I didn't realize how bad it was until I checked back into reality. The reality I had known before this chaos invaded my life. This was a whole new world, and my mind was abuzz with a curiosity about what else there could be out there, the world was so vast, so much untouched. What were we missing?

Carrie was driving us now, keeping Kyle and me in check as we missed and pined for Jax and Christian. Kyle took it hard, Jax had been like a brother to him, he felt shut out, we took it in turns reminding him it was for his own safety, but he always wrote that off. He felt abandonment.

We were driving up through the coastal towns that were reportedly still open but much of them had been evacuated, huge signs covered business doors, biblical reminders of the end, and some painting it for exactly what it was. *'The wolves are coming'*.

News had spread quickly and those brave enough to stay behind were racing about the streets as we passed through with guns and weapons to arm themselves and their property.

A voice inside me was screaming to jump out of the jeep and just run as far away as I could, but there was a new voice telling me to be brave and get to Cannon Beach.

"Kyle drive faster, we need to get to Cannon Beach," I urged.

"Why?" he asked.

"That's where Jax would have taken Christian to say goodbye to Noah," I sighed.

It wasn't facts, just instinct. That was where we all were the night it happened when we were pulling Jax into an ambulance with Kyle. When Noah disappeared into ash and Lupe lay lifeless in the sand, the weight of the world was finally off of her shoulders.

We pulled into Cannon Beach and a blood-curdling symphony of screaming welcomed us. It could be heard from multiple streets away and down the alley to the beach. Kyle grabbed his gun and raced for the beach, Carrie was packing the last two water guns we had and tossed me one, we were meters behind Kyle when we came to a sudden stop. The beach was strewn with bodies and hordes of werewolves were looking on as a fight between Jax, Christian, and two others unfolded.

Jax was in poor shape, every limb was dripping with blood from a wound, barely healing fast enough to keep up. He had his head down tearing into another werewolf, he was feasting and wild. Christian was in trouble; another werewolf was gnashing at his throat.

Kyle looked back, traded guns with Carrie, and sprinted into the middle to Christian's aid, he soaked the wolf in colloidal and it dropped to the sand with a loud thud as it cried in pain.

Then we saw Wesley, he was racing towards Kyle with a knife in his hand ready to plunge it into anything that got in his way, but he kicked Kyle to the ground, and pressed his face into the sand. We heard him inhale a mouthful of salty grit. He managed to flip over and grabbed Wesley's ankle and tore him down to the sand, but he landed on top of Kyle—and held the knife to his throat.

Seb was on the haystack now with his younger brothers holding them back.

I tore the gun from Carrie and raced down to Kyle as she yelled after me. I froze, I was stuck between Kyle and this evil man whose eyes were dark and sunken.

He barely resembled a human now, his face was pale, and it was obvious he hadn't slept in days, when he moved his lips they stuck first, tacky from dehydration. He was barely a man, he was crazed and living in fear of what he had become, but he was still just a man. Shakey and brittle, still trying to put his best foot forward as he challenged me with his towering height. But I wouldn't falter, I held the gun tighter, raised it to his chest and pressed it against him, and undid the safety.

"You don't have it in you," He laughed.

He pulled the knife away from Kyle and raised it towards me. The moon glimmered off the blade and he teased me with its movements. Kyle had a gash on his neck and Carrie raced to put pressure on the wound.

"Maybe I do! You're just one evil man, and the world will be better without you," I growled

"You wouldn't take a father from his children?" he teased.

"Your children will be better off without you. You're a coward and you're cruel. That's no role model for them," I snarled.

"Cruel?" He questioned.

"Look at what you've become, these are beasts, but they are also people with families, they aren't a part of this through faults of their own," I felt the heat in my chest as I fought through tears. Tears that belonged to Christian and all the others who stood here out of defense for those they loved.

"If you were going to pull, the trigger you'd have done it by now," he snickered as he grabbed the slide and tried to pull it away.

But Seb arose behind me, in his human form. Tears running down his cheeks, he pushed the gun back to his father but rose it to his forehead.

"You let us kill her, you hid, and only cared for yourself. Without beasts beside you, you are weak!" he whispered with a husky broken voice.

He forced Wesley to the ground and made him sit and watch as Jax carved his way through the masses of wolves that launched for him.

I released the gun to Seb and backed away to help Carrie. Kyle was ok, the gash wasn't deep enough to cause serious harm. We were bewildered to see so many werewolves tranced as they watched on, but they weren't watching the fight between humans, they were watching Jax and Christian feed on the pets that once accompanied Seb's father.

Jax was already tall, but his size grew with every wolf he devoured, he was picking them off and none of the others dare go near him, he had become a cannibal. He took too much pleasure in the feast, and Carrie was vomiting into the sea as she saw him rip ribs from the carcasses and strip them of flesh with one bite.

"Shoot them!" voices billowed from the haystack as survivors huddled in the brisk snow pouring down on us all. The night was getting colder, ice began to stick to the fur of the wolves and Seb anxiously stood over his father sobbing.

"Seb…" Carrie urged.

"I know, but he's the only parent I have left!" He growled at her as she pressed him to make that painful, but final call.

This man was too far gone, he'd seen too much, felt the poison of power and the weakness of loss. He was sobbing, but he was so dehydrated, nothing poured from his eyes, his cries rasp and dry, you could hear the scratching on his esophagus as screams evaded his body.

"Do it, Sebastian!" Wesley snapped.

His voice echoed between the rocks and Jax came to a halt from his frenzy and raced towards Seb.

Jax looked down at Wesley and roared. His eyes were completely red now, his muzzle drenched, a trail of blood dripped from his fur staining the snow and sand with every lift of his feet.

"Seb! No!" Mike called as he raced towards Wesley. Tristan chased after him as they leap over bodies and bones.

"That's my boy," Wesley smiled as Mike embraced him. Seb dropped the gun, fell to his knees, and held Mike and Wesley tightly.

"Jax!" Christian yelled. He was human again, covered in blood.

"Finish this, kill him!" Kyle growled.

"That's not for me to decide," Jax sighed.

Suddenly the loud shrieking energy of gunfire exploded through our eardrums.

Tristan had grabbed the gun and put a bullet through Wesley's head. The weight of his body fell onto Seb and Mike as they both disappeared into clouds of ash.

"Oh, shit!" Carrie shrieked.

Tristan dropped to the ground, and I rushed to catch him, and he broke into despair.

"We're going to look after you," I sighed as I brushed his hair back.

"What just happened?" Carrie asked as she looked around.

Puffs of ash began to appear, random werewolves dropped to the sand and carcasses vanished.

"He was their leader…" Jax mumbled in amazement.

"But how? he was human?" Christian interjected.

"Wesley controlled Seb, Mike, and Tristan. Others they turned would have followed their lead. He was inevitably the top of the ladder," I interrupted.

"Then why am I still alive?" Tristan asked.

"You killed him, when Seb and Mike felt mercy, you stood against them.

There were five others left on the beach who hadn't been taken out with Wesley, they immediately turned back into humans and knelt as Jax paced before each of them.

"Who are you?" Jax asked as he wiped his newly growing beard free from the chunks of flesh.

"We weren't with them, we are residents who lived in those houses," He pointed beyond the trees.

They had no blood on them, no evidence of being exposed to the hunger that ensnared the others.

People began climbing down from the haystack as the tide went out. The moon faded away and the early morning sun shed its light on yet another massacre.

The bloodbath in the ocean disappeared with the sharks and marine life and the people brave enough waded into the freezing water and rushed to shore.

Some ran and clung to the men who had been turned, others raced to the street, desperate to return to their homes, desperate for warmth and for this nightmare to end.

"We can't let them go!" I yelled at Christian as he watched them walk away huddling together through the sand.

"Yes, we can…" he sighed

"They know about you all, they know what you look like!" Carrie scowled as she pulled Kyle up.

"Everyone knows now Carrie, we can't cover this up anymore it's too far gone, we have to leave," Jax sighed.

"What?" I snapped.

"Where will you go?" Kyle asked.

"Yukon, where we can't harm or turn anyone else, there's nothing there and that means no risk," Christian gently held my hand as Jax explained this to us, but only held my gaze.

"We'll come too," one of the men announced as they all nodded.

"We don't attack humans," Jax paced once more making it a firm rule.

"And the only way to take down another werewolf is to feed on their bodies till there is nothing left, or kill the leader they serve," he added.

"That's what you were doing? Keeping the most dangerous of them down?" I questioned.

"Wesley had starved two of them to the point of complete insanity, they weren't going to be human again," Christian replied.

"If Tristan hadn't taken control of the situation, we'd all be dead," Kyle smiled as he held Tristan's shoulder.

"Thank you, Tristan," I hugged him again.

His face was sad, defeated but full of relief.

"Seb would have been swayed by dad, Mike would follow, I couldn't live that way, doing his bidding," he sobbed.

"You're safe with us now, but we should go before anyone finds us," Jax said.

"Come and get some clothes, supplies, some real food. Then we'll all leave together," One of the men said.

He was easily in his forties, sweeping dark hair and bright blue eyes with a wife clinging to his side.

"Thank you, what's your name?" I asked.

"Henry, this is Izzy," he introduced his wife.

"Thank you. Let's go everyone!" Jax announced as we all followed Henry.

Chapter Nine

Christian

The newer members each went to their homes to collect their supplies and pack their belongings into their cars.

"Jax, we can't bring their families, this will breed trouble," I sighed.

"Don't they deserve to try?" he asked.

"Try to what? Snack on their wives? their kids? you're suddenly singing a different tune!" I growled.

"They might not be like you Christian, they might be able to control themselves," he snarled.

"What the fuck does that mean," I shoved him against Henry's garage door.

"I saw your eyes turn orange out there…I've only seen that on werewolves who have completely lost control. You fed too much!" He yelled into my face as he pressed me back onto a car.

"Your eyes were red Jax! I've never seen that one before. Have you?" I questioned.

"Woah, guys…let's take a breath," Kyle emerged from the house with a bandage around his neck.

"Can you control it, Jax?" I launched for Kyle gripped him by the shirt and tore the bandage from his neck as I pressed the wound to Jax's face.

"Christian!" Celinde screamed as she desperately tried to pull Kyle from between Jax and me.

"What the fuck Christian!" Kyle yelled as he picked himself up from the ground.

Jax's eyes were red, his claws were sunken into the body of a car, gripping, desperate to hold himself back.

"You have more self-control than I thought…" I sighed.

He was panting as he lowered his head to hide his eyes.

"Jax, are you okay?" Kyle whispered.

His hands wiped over his face as his claws retracted back into his hands, his body still covered in bruising, blood, and sand.

"Hey Jax, how about a hot shower?" Henry called out from the door as he held a plush folded towel.

"Thanks, Henry," Jax accepted and claimed the towel and entered the home.

He quickly made his way through the halls for the bathroom.

"It's been a rough night," Henry sighed.

"Rough life," Kyle replied with a forced smile.

"Come in, get comfy. Izzy is making some breakfast for us all," Henry gave Tristan a friendly pat on the back to go and sit at the table.

Henry was a warm person. He brought out beers, juice, water, and his wife Izzy grilled sausages, bacon, and eggs.

"Let's go help her," Celinde nudged Carrie.

She wouldn't look at me, I'd pushed her, I'd pushed everyone and to them I was unreasonable, but my thoughts were only of her safety, I knew if Henry's wife came, she'd come, and others would bring their wives and children.

I would raise hell before I let harm near her, I was desperate to take harm completely out of the equation, but the only answer was to remove Celinde.

Smells wafted from the kitchen as the girls cooked the contents of the large fridge. I claimed a beer and went to sit with Tristan and Kyle.

"I'm sorry man. That was too far," I apologized.

"He could have taken my head off you do realize that?" Kyle was pissed.

"But he didn't," I replied.

"Not the point," He argued.

"I'm not going to fight with you too, I'm sorry. It won't happen again," I sighed as I slumped back into a chair.

Celinde started filling the dining table with plates of food and Tristan was quick to wander over and start sneaking rashers of bacon.

"Grab a plate," Izzy smiled as she filled his hands with cutlery and a large plate full of buttery toast.

"There are towels in the cupboard beside the bathroom. Help yourselves to whatever you need," she smiled with tired eyes.

It was reasonable to wonder if her hospitality was out of fear or purely genuine. She was a southern lady with an accent that had real strength to it, a short dark pixie haircut, and bright green eyes.

"Thanks, Izzy," Carrie hugged her.

"We're all in this together now," she smiled.

The sound of it enraged me, that we would be moving to the middle of nowhere and Jax was suddenly letting everyone bring their families. I sunk the beer fast and went to eat some food as I waited for Jax to come out from the shower.

"Here's some clean clothes," Henry dumped a pile of winterwear onto the couch and raced to the table to snap up a plate of food. He softly kissed his wife as she clung to him tightly.

She gazed into his eyes and examined his changes, his eyes bright and slightly bloodshot, skin now dry and red bumps covered him from the harshness of the bristly fur. He held her hand as it brushed over him.

"I'm fine, darling," he kissed her soft pout.

Celinde locked my gaze as she caught me watching them as she sat across from me, her eyes dark, tired but stronger than the last time I saw her. She had hardened from the gentle woman she was before we entered that tunnel, the way she held my hand and felt every hair, vein, and knuckle like they were hers. That gentle, shy woman was just a memory.

I stabbed my fork into a sausage on her plate and stole it to soften the mood between us.

"So, you're coming on the road trip too?" I asked.

"If Carrie is going, so am I…" She replied.

"Well, I'm staying with Kyle, and Kyle isn't leaving Jax alone with you after that stunt," Carrie sneered at me.

"What, are you two a thing now?" I asked jokingly.

"Maybe we are," Kyle kissed her on the cheek and Carrie freaked and looked at Celinde with a worried look.

"Aww!" Izzy smiled.

"I remember the honeymoon phase, it's magical, enjoy it and steal every moment, cuddle and kiss you can grasp," she added as placed down another plate of toast.

"It's not like that for all of us…" Celinde sighed.

I knew what she meant, she was right to feel that way, but I couldn't understand how she didn't see that all I was doing was trying to protect her.

"Showers free!" Jax announced as he entered the dining room in a towel.

"There are clothes here," Henry patted the pile.

"Although I don't know if I have anything that'll fit you!" he chuckled as he poked at Jax's biceps and pecks.

"I'll make do, thank you," he smiled.

I grabbed a towel from the hallway and ran a hot shower to clean off all the blood. The heat filled the room with a cloud of steam and then I heard the door creak. I pulled the curtain back and Celinde placed down a towel and began to remove her clothes. I pulled her into the shower and our lips found one another.

"It's only because I can't stand the thought of you unhappy or in harm's way," I gushed into her mouth as she focused her eyes on patches of dried blood on my chest.

"You can't attack our friends over it, Jax isn't to blame here. He's trying to create an environment of safety for all of us," She scolded.

"Well, if he fucks it up, I'll kill him," I laughed.

"So, I can come?" she smiled, and she wrapped her arms around my neck.

"Do I have a choice?" I kissed her softly.

"What happened tonight won't ever happen again Christian," she stroked my cheek.

"You don't know that" I sighed.

"I do," she growled.

She pressed her finger against my lips stopping me from talking. I poured body wash into a loofah and lathered her body with it, she returned the favor by scrubbing off the sand and blood, taking her time over the red and bruised areas.

I lathered her hair with shampoo, her back against my chest as she gently ground the crevice of her ass against me.

"Not here," I chuckled.

"I know… there are others waiting for the shower," she sighed as she held me in her hands and kissed me deeply as the force of the water washed the suds out of her hair.

"Stop pushing me away Christian…I can't take much more of your rejection," she saddened her gaze.

"It's not from a lack of care, it's because I care too much," I confessed.

"Come on!" Tristan slammed his fists on the door.

"Alright, we're done," I turned off the water and we wrapped ourselves in towels and dressed in some of the clothes Henry had left out.

The others took turns with the shower and once breakfast was over, we prepped as best as we could, gathering blankets, food, and supplies from Henry's home and those only half incinerated, already abandoned and lost to the fires that illuminated the beach last night.

Other survivors who had been turned were driving down the hill to Henry's home and began piling out of their cars to formally meet us all.

Izzy was introducing Carrie and Celinde to two other women, Kitty and Mindy. Kitty was married to a welder by the name of Jake. Mindy to Arthur, they had a young daughter named Alexa.

There were also two bachelors, Jamal who was about my age, and Otis who was likely the oldest of us all, he was grey and had a concerning amount of beer stacked up in the back of his car. Jamal was riding with him; they had a large white Nissan patrol with all the fixings of outdoorsy life already in place.

"Good call on the four-wheeler," I grimaced as I shook their hands.

"Yukon isn't the place for Tesla's or corvettes," Jamal chuckled.

"What do we do with the fire truck? We can't keep it, it's too thirsty for gas," Carrie questioned.

"Leave it, we've got two cars, might as well take them both," Henry offered.

"Thank you," Jax patted him on the back.

"Do the girls all want to go together? These are uncertain times for all of us, it might be better for everyone's safety?" Arthur asked as he held his wife and daughter.

"Absolutely! We might as well get to know each other. Canada is a long drive from here," Carrie smiled as she went to meet Alexa.

"How long is the drive?" Alexa asked in a sweet voice.

"It's going to take a few days," Kyle jumped up to meet her and make her feel welcome.

"Has everyone got enough warm clothes and blankets?" Jax asked.

"Blankets and beers," smiled Otis.

"Food? Tents? Bear spray? Batteries, building equipment?" I pondered loudly.

"We'll take what we need, for now. Building equipment, we can get closer to Yukon," Jax answered.

"There are old, abandoned bunkers for sale out there. If we pool our money, we might find one big enough?" Arthur explained.

Everyone around nodded in agreement and Carrie set to work looking online for bunkers available for purchase.

We all climbed into our cars and the girls into the jeep.

My phone buzzed; it was Carrie.

"Okay, forget Yukon. There's a large bunker in Alberta and it's away from any towns. Willmore, it's beautiful there and has a river and open glades. The bunker has three wings with family-sized rooms. Plus, it's way closer than Yukon!" Carrie explained as we drove north.

"What's in the other wing?" I asked.

"Kitchen, infirmary. I think it's ex-government," she added.

"I'll run it by the boss and catch you up once we hit the first rest stop," I hung up the phone and turned to Jax.

"She's pretty darn fast!" Jax chuckled.

"She's definitely savvy," I agreed.

"So, we all have that supersonic hearing thing? I don't need to relay the message?" I asked.

"Not a thing…" Jax sneered.

"You know why they put us alone in this truck together don't you?" I mumbled.

"So, we could work out our differences," Jax answered.

"I just don't want any more casualties…least of all Celinde, Carrie, or Kyle. I've come to be very fond of you all," I sighed.

"We all know how fond of Celinde you are," Jax laughed.

"She's changed, Jax," I sighed with worry.

"What do you mean?" he asked.

"She's hardened against me; she's pushing back now, and I think it could go awry," I explained.

"I understand and I'm sorry for the discomfort and uncertainty that all of our new companions bring you, but they aren't safe either. They are connections to all of us. If someone went looking, they are the first stop.

It's important we protect them too, whether or not they are like us," Jax gloomed.

I knew he was right. Warrenton and Astoria had already been wiped out and by more than just werewolves, our kind had been exterminated. Probably by the government and they likely had taken a sampling—one of us that could undermine all the rest.

There was chatter between Otis and Arthur of some activity in Washington. I doubted anyone would be up for chasing another deadly lead. Jax's goal seemed to be to get everyone who was manageable to safety and salvage what we could of seemingly normal lives.

"Alberta?" I huffed.

"It's not Yukon, but if it's got a safe place to lock down when one or all of us aren't in control then we'll work with it. Beats starting from scratch with logs and chainsaws," he expressed.

"I can't say I was too keen on building anything the minute we arrived. Carrie's probably already set it all up with furniture and a full fridge, that girl's organizational skills are unrivaled," I laughed.

"She's a huge help—and stupid smart. Kyle's just too proud to admit that after all these years she's caught his attention," Jax sighed.

"Maybe I should have shoved him into her..." I grunted.

"She would have kicked your ass and you know it," Jax smiled.

"Yep, she's fierce. It's that flaming red hair. She's terrifying some days, werewolf or not, I wouldn't mess with her," I laughed.

"What do you think of the rest of our company so far?" Jax enquired.

"They all seem pretty open to this new life. I could smell the fear on Mindy and Alexa though, I think that's why Arthur put them in the Jeep with the girls. He might even be worried he'll snap," I sighed.

"We need to be strong and look out for them all, we have more experience," Jax ordered.

"You were right about me, I lost control last night," I shuddered as I recalled the events that took place.

"It was one time, you'll be okay. I'm more worried about Tristan, he's still grieving, and he's taken a liking to you and Kyle. That's fine and all, but Kyle is human, and he's expressed he'd like to stay that way," Jax explained.

"I don't think he'd harm him," I added.

"Tristan is used to feeding on humans, constantly. It wouldn't matter who it was," Jax gulped.

"Maybe at the next stop we fill everyone up with food, and we swap cars. Tristan can ride with me and Kyle with you," I asked.

"I think that's a good idea. We've been driving for hours. Celinde will be getting hangry any second now," I added.

"We aren't far from Kamloops, we'll get a place for the night there," Jax decided.

CHAPTER TEN

JAX

We pulled into the Hue Hotel. I walked into reception to book seven rooms for us all.

I went out to distribute keys amongst our companions and made swift dinner plans. Every obvious couple paired off and went to their rooms to rest before we were to meet.

"Tristan, you got me," I nudged as I handed him the key to run ahead.

"Thanks, Jax," he nodded as he sprinted ahead.

It came to my attention that Tristan had no belongings of his own, no clothes other than the torn ones he wore, or the oversized shirts and pants Henry had given him the whole time he had been with us and for a teenager of 19, his appearance probably meant something to him.

"Are you tired Trist?" I asked.

"Somewhat…" he yawned.

"Get some sleep. By the way, what size do you wear?" I smiled.

"Medium shirts and pants, size 11 shoes," he answered with warmth to his expression.

"Roger that, bud!" I chirped.

"Jax!" He called before I could close the hotel door.

"Yeah?" I answered.

"I haven't really had a chance to say thank you," he sighed.

"For what?" I squinted.

"For looking out for me, for helping me. For seeing the good in me and not condemning me to a fate like my brothers or madness like my father," he sobbed.

I sat on the bed beside him and allowed him his moment of grief, I knew all too well that sometimes it helped just to cry to someone even if they couldn't console me.

"I'm sorry about your family Tristan, none of that should've ever happened to any of you," I sighed as I watched him cry into his hands.

"I miss them…" he heaved.

"I understand your pain, I lost my girlfriend and little brother to this also," tears welled in my eyes, but I dare not let them fall past my cheeks.

"Where do you find the strength?" he begged.

"I try not to think about it. There are others, like you and Christian who need my strength a lot more. My time will come, and I know it'll hit me like a thousand daggers to my heart, but I have all the time in the world to feel that pain. Right now, I need to do what I can to keep you all safe and others safe from us, I'm just a control freak, even where my grief is concerned. I won't be ruled by it," I confessed.

"But I am," he sulked.

"Tristan, my control has been my savior in all of this, and you have your own strengths. You proved that when you stood against the others and weren't turned into ash," I patted him on the back as he wiped his sorrows with a tissue.

"Lycanthropy suits you," he laughed.

"It's going to have to unless you have a cure in your back pocket," I laughed back.

"Do you think there is one?" I asked.

"If this is possible, there's gotta be more," he smiled with optimism.

"I'm going to go and get some snacks and clothes for us. You wanna come?" I asked.

"Yeah, why not! Not like I'll be able to sleep with my mind buzzing about that now," he agreed.

We grabbed the keys and headed down to the cars and drove over to Costco. Carrie and Kyle were already inside devouring a whole pizza when Tristan sprung up behind them and stole a slice.

"Oh good! You're here, I just got a call from the realtor about the bunker, he's going to drop the keys off to us there. Along with an apparently large photographic file of directions and instructions that we'll have to study," she finished with a deep sigh.

"So, when can we move in?" I asked.

"Tonight…tomorrow, your call," she added.

"Everyone grab a cart," I nodded.

"Each of us?" Kyle was miffed.

"Yes, we're going to need a lot of food, it's still a few hours' drive from here," I replied.

"Lucky it's freezing then, and everything should be good till we get there," Carrie smiled.

"Tristan, you're on beverages, Carrie you've got bread and vegetables, Kyle you're on meat, I'll get pantry goods. We'll have to make a second trip for laundry, clothing, and all the rest," I sighed knowing I was yet again going to get absolutely no sleep.

"You're so annoying dude," Kyle yawned as he sped off riding his cart, feet on the wheels and half a slice of pizza hanging from his teeth.

"You'll be thanking me when it's you who gets to pick out king crab and steaks from the fridges," I called back.

Kyle was much like Joel in his expensive eating habits. Joel would have loved this and made the most of the comradery we had built. Shopping always reminded me of Joel, and it felt wrong to do it without him. His useless appliances that he'd sneak into the cart, most still unopened in my garage that I'll never see again. He'd have taken control here and had lists for every member of our new family down to the way it would all be packed into the vehicles. I missed him, so much more than I allowed myself to feel.

Maybe it was Tristan who reminded me that feeling all these things were normal, expected, and okay. I couldn't keep staggering my grief, I'd hit rock bottom that way, once everyone was set up, I had a plan.

"Jax!" Kyle yelled as he held up two packs of Dungeness crabs.

"You'll need more than that," I smiled from a distance.

"Right!" He began hauling packets of seafood and assorted other meats into his cart.

This was the first time I'd been shopping since the chaos occurred and it was the most normal, I'd felt and probably would feel for a long time to come.

"Don't look, but I think we've been followed," Carrie whispered as she hugged me gently to disguise her panic.

I looked about and eyes of inhumane shades were on me, these weren't wolves who belonged to our group.

"Shh," I hushed Carrie.

If they were like us, they'd hear every word we spoke. Hesitation and fear were feelings I couldn't afford to linger in the air about us.

We kept our heads down as we finished the shopping and checked out. They always stayed several meters away from us—but were always in sight. Three of them if I was counting them correctly. One was short with thick blonde hair, another with bright red hair, eyes yellow and bulging, he likely had only just learnt to control himself, but his yellow eyes gave me hope. The other had long brown strands strung into a bun on top of his head, and dressed like we were in Hawaii, certainly not prepared for the frost of Kamloops.

Tristan was filling the car with Carrie and Kyle and collected the carts.

"Quite a haul you got there," smiled the yellowed eyed ginger man.

"Austin," he reached his hand with claws sprung from his nail beds.

"Jax," I offered mine.

"You know, you should probably dial back the werewolf stuff," I suggested as I held onto his hand.

"Don't worry, we're friendlies. We came from Hurricane Ridge," he sighed.

"Hurricane? That's where I was turned too," Tristan exclaimed as he walked over.

"That was a pretty terrible morning," Austin sighed.

"This is Liam and Ezra," he introduced.

Liam was the blonde, he had the same yellow eyes and not a lot to say, his skin was scabbed and red from the cold. Ezra was more put together, he resembled a large biker, well out of touch with the other two who looked more like college dropouts. His eyes were mostly white, tan skin and he had locked his gaze on Carrie as she smiled like the hopeless romantic, we all knew she was.

Kyle rolled his as at her as he ignored the chatter between Austin and Tristan.

"Do you guys have a base?" I asked.

"Mostly national parks, places we can be free to be ourselves," Ezra answered.

"Are there more of you," Carrie was quick to interject.

"Just us, pretty lady," Ezra was smooth with his words and Carrie was lapping it up like a kitten.

"But you've seen others?" She asked.

"Yes, and we quickly learned to stay away from them, most can't be trusted," he grunted.

"Where will you go?" Liam asked.

"We bought a bunker away from any towns, we're moving there tomorrow," I explained.

"There's a few of us, if you are who you say you are, you're welcome to join us," I expressed.

"How many?" Ezra asked.

"15, some human," I replied.

"And you two are humans? And you're going too?" He looked at Kyle and Carrie.

"We lost everything back in Warrenton, this is our family now," Kyle replied as he rested his arm on Carrie's shoulder protectively.

"We're staying at the Hue, come by for dinner, meet the rest of us and then decide. If you don't want to join us, we respect that," I went to shake Ezra's hand.

"Let's go!" Kyle urged.

I climbed into the car as we watched our three new companions jump into a large four-wheeler.

"You don't like him," I snickered.

"Do you?" Kyle growled.

"They seem okay, I couldn't smell human blood on them, mostly moose," I shuddered.

"You know what I mean, that guy is dripping with sex, and he has eyes for Carrie," he grunted.

"She's tried with you for years, now you're shitty. Should she just flirt with you and do your washing forever and not move on?" I chuckled.

"Did she tell you she does my washing?" he gasped.

"She does everyone's washing!" I laughed.

"Fuck…" he sighed.

"Maybe Ezra was the push you needed," I sneered.

"He's huge, and a werewolf, don't we have enough of those relationship problems with Celinde and Christian?" he asked.

"Yep, what's one more," I gulped.

"Look, if you like her, do something. Now!" I pointed to her as we rolled into a parking bay.

Kyle leapt from the car and raced after Carrie as she entered the hotel doors.

"Tristan!" I yelled as I pulled him back.

"Don't worry, we can listen from here," I smiled.

"Oh, not them too!" He sighed.

"Don't worry, I'm done with that stuff, we'll be bachelors together," I nudged as he laughed in response.

We watched on as Kyle threw himself at Carrie's feet and she looked at him with intense confusion.

"Carrie, I care for you…" he beamed.

"Are you kidding me, Kyle?" she asked quietly.

"I thought we could try dating?" he suggested.

"Kyle, how many times have you rejected my advances?" she crossed her arms as a shadow of sadness wavered between them.

"I was wrong…" he sighed.

"No, you weren't. But right now, things are new and lonely. Don't mistake that loneliness as affection for me. We've got a good thing going here, we've become good friends. Let's not ruin that," she sighed and offered a friendly hug.

"Ohhh shit," Tristan blurted from the carpark.

"Okay," Kyle replied and rejected her advances for a hug. He was embarrassed, confused and hurt.

Carrie took the stairs up to her room and he sat there knelt on the floor for the moments it took us to reach him.

"Great advice, Jax!" He growled.

"I didn't know how she would react; she's never been that mature about men," I grumbled in confusion.

"I would have dated you, Kyle," Tristan smiled.

"Shut up, Tristan!" Kyle scowled.

Kyle was embarrassed and stroppy and raced off to his room, the same room he was meant to be sharing with Carrie.

We followed him up to the floor we were all booked on and Carrie and Christian were in the hall swapping their baggage into each other's rooms.

"You got me for the night," Christian hesitated as he met Kyle's gaze.

Christian darted me a concerned look as Carrie quickly shut the door behind her and Celinde winced a sleepy stare at Christian.

"Well, that escalated quickly. Does anyone care to fill me in?" Christian glowered as he pulled his pants on and hauled his luggage out of the door.

Kyle went into the room and slammed the door shut.

"Come in here," I ordered.

Christian entered the room and Tristan explained to him the details of what happened in comedic depth. Tristan had a young vibrance we truly needed amongst us, he kept everything upbeat and entertaining, but I always worried for him, his loss far exceeded the rest of ours.

"Woah…" Christian gushed.

"How did you guys get two queen beds?" He stammered as he looked around our room.

"Well, I gave you the key to the single trying to help you out, did it help?" I asked.

"It did," he said with grace to his voice.

"And now I'm stuck with Kyle, in another single room," he added.

"Okay, that didn't work out, go and book another room if you want," I said as I handed him some cash.

"No, the poor guys had enough rejection for one day," he laughed.

"Do you think Carrie is interested in this Ezra guy?" He asked.

"You should have felt the sexual tension," Tristan gagged.

"He's the perfect specimen if you're into rugged, body of a demigod and a deep raspy voice sharper than my claws," I enthused.

"Are you sure you don't have the hots for him?" Christian laughed.

"Dude, just wait…" Tristan added to back me up.

"Damn, I'm going to have to keep Celinde tied up," he laughed.

"So that's going well?" I asked.

"It's been a journey, but we got there," he sighed.

Christian headed back to his room and Tristan went for a wander to knock on everyone's doors to tell them all to meet for dinner at 6:30 down at Brownstones.

I went down to the parking lot first. Austin, Liam, and Ezra were there and dressed slightly better. They all had their eyes under better control.

"Hey Jax," Austin smiled as he greeted me.

"Glad you guys chose to join us," I nodded as we leant on the cars and waited for the others.

Mindy, Alexa, and Arthur came down first and I introduced them to the newcomers. Kitty and Jake came down with Izzy and Henry and moments later Jamal and Otis followed with the others.

"Everyone, this is Liam, Austin, and Ezra. They are like us, they'll be joining us for dinner," I smiled as Kitty clung to Carrie and smiled as she devoured Ezra with her eyes.

"None of the girls are werewolves?" Austin asked.

"None of us have ever come across a female werewolf," Christian answered as he stepped forward beside me.

"Neither have we…" I replied.

"Natures got a sick sense of humor," Ezra sighed as he gloomed in Carrie's direction.

"It sure does," Celinde sighed as she held onto Christian, it was obvious she felt uneasy around so many newcomers.

"Well, I'm famished! Let's get some dinner," Mindy smiled trying to break the mood.

"Yes! I'm starving," Otis agreed.

Once at the restaurant Kyle made a beeline for the bar and ordered a round of beers.

"Can I have five raspberry ciders," Carrie asked over the bar. She was trying not to make eye contact with Kyle.

Ezra sat at the table chatting with Jamal and Tristan. Carrie sat across from him with Kitty and Celinde to each side of her.

Kyle sat at the other end of the table with Otis, Arthur, Henry, and Jake.

"How many rare steaks am I ordering?" I asked.

Every wolf raised his hand and smiled at the inside joke I'd made. The comradery was genuine, something about being a werewolf and sharing it with others instead of punishing them for it was warm and rewarding and I felt we would find a way to make this work.

The girls mostly ordered fish and chicken dishes and a healthy stream of cocktails seemed to be constantly flowing between them.

"So, what were you, in your past life?" I asked the new guys.

"Plumber," Liam replied.

"Teacher," Austin answered.

"Mechanic, but I was logging for the last three years," Ezra replied.

"Yourself?" Austin asked.

"Surgeon," replied.

"What about you?" Ezra smiled at Carrie.

"Paramedic," she smiled girlishly.

The table went around, and we had a huge variety of people in our company. Firefighters, police, medics, teachers, florists, interior decorators, hotel owners, and a variety of other professions.

Chapter Eleven

Carrie

Dinner seemed to never end and as much as I was enjoying shamelessly flirting with Ezra, Jax and Christian were hovering over me like big brothers in defense of Kyle.

I knew he was feeling deflated and rejected, probably emasculated as he was the only human male here. Something he cherished above all else, he took a lot of pride in being mine and Celinde's protector in times when Jax and Christian were lost and out of control.

But, if we were all going to live together, then we needed to be honest and not have secrets, I had held up my end of that by being blatantly open with him about how I felt. Celinde was devasted, it was hard to tell if it were because she had hoped for double dates hiking through the mountains or me kicking Christian out of his room and into mine.

Christian was good for her, he challenged her. She had never had that kind of passion in her life. She dated the safe guys, the ones who drank five coffee's a day and had the same lunch every day for work. Christian was takeout to her, and she was addicted.

Ezra's ankle was against mine beneath the table, he oozed excitement and intensity, and he made me feverish with his short, but deep glances, his eyes were deeper than the ocean and I was lost in them. I must have been flushed just from his aroma; he made my head spin.

"Join me outside?" he whispered over the table.

I got up from the table and we went to the courtyard, he followed behind me and felt the eyes of the whole table follow us also.

"I can't say much, not without the rest of the pack hearing," he chuckled.

"Now I'm curious! What did you want to say to me?" I smiled.

"I'll just show you," he smiled and placed his arms around my waist, and I seemed to fit perfectly in his embrace. He was warm even though the night was cold, and snowflakes fell on our cheeks and disappeared just as quickly from our warmth.

He pressed his lips gently onto mine and I succumbed to him as I gently pulled him into me, my arms knotted around his neck.

"We aren't going to upset Kyle are we," he pulled back with a seriousness.

"I chased Kyle for years. By the time he felt what I once felt, it was too late," sighed.

"Ugh, the friendzone," he sighed.

"Yeah, I don't think Jax is so happy with me," I shuddered from a breeze of cold wind.

"Jax seems like a good man, I think he'll be the voice of reason," he held me tighter.

"He'll be fine. Everything is new and different right now," I admitted.

"How long have they all been werewolves?" He asked.

"Not long, some just turned a few nights ago, others much longer," I replied.

"And you?" I added.

"Ten years…" he sighed.

"That's a long time! Longer than Noah," I pondered loudly.

"Who's Noah?" He asked.

"He was the first werewolf any of us knew of, he was Jax' girlfriends' husband...he was also Christian's best friend," I explained.

"That sounds messy," he sighed.

"Very, Jax lost his brother, Joel in the same night," I confessed.

"It's a nasty life at times, I find it's best to keep a low profile, fit in where I can, and control my diet with animals, the rawer, the better," he smiled.

"Hence the two rare steaks," I laughed.

"Yep," he laughed back.

"How do you know Austin and Liam?" I asked.

"I heard about the bodies piling up down in Washington, I went to check it out. After the massacre at Hurricane Ridge, I gathered who I could, who was still of sound mind, and saw reason, there were a lot who didn't, the forest was thick with them, Liam and Austin helped me tear the bodies apart and burn them. Werewolves are extremely hard to kill, some got away," he sighed.

"Home time, Carebear!" Jax announced as he opened the door.

"Sorry, snow's coming down heavy now," he apologized for interrupting.

"I'll be seeing you," Ezra smiled as he pecked me on the cheek.

"I've given Austin the details. The more hands the better," Jax nodded.

"See you tomorrow then?" I smiled.

"Guess so," he agreed.

Jax held the door open for us and lead us to the exit.

The next day was brighter, the snow had passed.

Tristan and Henry were outside trying to melt the snow off the windshields.

"At least we know the food is going to be fine," Celinde smiled from the window as we watched from the comfort of the heater.

"Carrie, are you sure you know what you're doing?" Celinde asked.

"Cel, Kyle's been rejecting me for years! And the one time I do it everyone's acting like I smacked a puppy," I sighed.

"Okay fair...he just needs more than a friend right now," she pressed.

"He's got hands Celinde, he won't diminish from lack of sex. He's also the only male who can go galivanting as he pleases, he isn't a threat like the others," I huffed.

"No, he won't but he might become jealous if you do…" she nudged.

"So, leave you and Christian to have all the fun?" I snickered.

"Yes, I see what you mean. Ezra is quite a hunk, and he seems lovely! Just don't rub it in Kyle's face please," she begged.

"I would never intentionally hurt him," I assured her.

I collected my bag and headed down to the cars.

"Good morning girls!" Henry beamed.

"Morning Henry," I smiled.

"Jax and Jamal went with Jake and Kitty to get the rest of the shopping, they said we should get a head start, there's a dirt track into the mountains. Ezra knows it well, he'll guide us," He began.

"The rest should be down soon," he smiled.

"Where are the others then if they are leading the way?" I asked.

"Should be here any minute," he answered.

Ezra, Liam, and Austin all rolled up in their four-wheeler and handed us cup trays of hot coffees.

"Ohhh! I approve, forget everything I said," Celinde was smitten as she grabbed the tray and inhaled the scent of coffee as the steam warmed her face.

"That was erotic," Austin laughed.

Celinde ignored his comment as she guzzled her coffee as if she were immune to the searing hot temperature.

"Is that not hot?" I asked.

"Not when your whole body is frozen. I feel nothing, not even my tongue!" she winced.

Christian rushed down the stairs and hauled his bag into one of the cars and claimed a cup of coffee and reveled in it the same way Celinde had.

"Coffee people!" Arthur laughed as he ignored the tray.

"Not a coffee man?" Austin asked.

"I'm British," he snuffed.

"Brilliant! I'll have yours," Celinde cheered as she took a second cup.

"No, one's enough! You will shit yourself before we get to the bunker," I exclaimed.

"You are foul, Carrie!" she cried as I placed the second coffee back.

"No, I'm a realist, and I have to share a car with you," I laughed.

"Woah, they're fun!" Liam said excitably.

"They're savages, worse than werewolves…" Kyle laughed as he took a dig at me. He then grabbed a coffee from the tray on the bonnet.

Jax and the others finally rolled up with a boot full of more goods from Costco.

"Is everyone ready to go?" He asked from the window.

"Yep, let's hit it!" Ezra smiled as he handed them a tray full of coffees.

"Okay let's roll," Austin smiled.

The girls all stuck together and we rode in the same car as we had done on the way up from Cannon Beach.

It was a few more hours Northeast from Kamloops.

"Who's Kyle riding with?" Celinde asked quietly.

"I saw him jump in with Jax and Christian," Kitty answered.

"How are you doing with all that Carrie?" Mindy questioned.

"Ugh, it's common knowledge I assume?" I asked.

"Oh yeah…Christian told Henry at dinner he had to bunk with Kyle, and he wasn't exactly thrilled about it," she sighed with a sympathetic tone.

"I never meant to give him the wrong impression," I grumbled as I drove the car tightly behind Henry and Jake's.

"For what it's worth I never saw you flirt or give off seductive impressions," Mindy rubbed my shoulder from behind me.

"Thanks, Mindy. It's been a hard few months for Kyle, I think a lot of this stems from me being familiar in a time when we've all lost so much," I sighed.

"Your presence was somewhere he found comfort," Celinde squeezed my hand.

"He'll be okay! Jax is his best friend, right?" Izzy asked.

"Yeah, since childhood," Celinde replied.

"He'll get over it," Kitty grimaced.

"Tell us about the bunker? Henry said there's a mess hall?" Mindy asked.

"Yes! There are three wings, it's not a multi-level bunker. Two housing wings and the other has the kitchen, laundry, mess, greenhouse, and gym. Don't expect it to be clean though, hence the price tag being so low. The agents meeting us there at midday," I explained.

"The guys got cleaning products and such right?" Izzy asked.

"I saw Jax with two vacuums and some mop buckets. He's pretty organized," I assured them.

"He is the nicest man and so hot! what's his story?" Kitty asked.

Kitty was giving me problematic vibes, she and Jake always seemed edgy around one another, and she wasn't shy about pointing out how hot Ezra was and now Jax. Celinde must have caught a whiff of it too, her eyes lowered and caught mine as I gently rolled my eyes to myself.

"Jax is awesome, eternally single, and broken-hearted," Celinde interrupted loud and defensively.

She was making a statement, we'd both come to be very protective of Jax, he had done the same for us and that was family now. Kitty's intentions didn't seem pure, she was constantly fixing her hair, applying gloss, and acting more like a teenager on heat than an adult with marital problems.

"I'm sure he'll get over it…" Kitty smirked.

"The heart wants, what the heart wants. He's had a rough trot, might be best to leave him alone Kitty, and divert your attention to fixing things with Jake," Mindy huffed.

"Woah…" I choked. I knew Mindy was a lot more forthcoming, she was the mama bear I always wanted, and if she had claws, they just sunk right into Kitty's throat.

"What do you know Mindy? Town gossip!" Kitty growled.

"

"I know you Kitty Flores and I saw you on your wedding night chatting up Matthew Barns," Mindy yelled.

"Okay, I'm pulling over, they can have this out on the road…" I said to Celinde.

"Mama!" Alexa screamed. Kitty had pulled Mindy's hair, Izzy stuck in the middle and Alexa sitting in the boot saw the whole thing.

I pulled the car over into the dirt and jumped out to open their doors and pull them both out. Izzy climbed out and stood beside Celinde and me. The others pulled over up ahead and ran back down the road to see what the problem was.

The road was alive with yelling and screaming and poor Jake knew none of what was being let out into the air.

"What's going on?" Jax asked.

"Too many hours together…" I expressed with a sigh.

"What in the hell?" Jake asked as he pulled Mindy and Kitty apart.

"You married the town bicycle. I'm sorry Jake, but that whore is sitting around rating every man here like it's hot or not and I know she cheats on you!" Mindy yelled.

"Oh, dear god…" Jax growled.

"We don't have time for this nonsense, Mindy, get in with us," Henry ordered.

Mindy stormed off and Kitty lowered her head as she climbed back into the car. Alexa raced after her mom and hoped into their car as Jake came and jumped in with us.

"You sure you don't want to jump in with Otis and Jamal?" Kitty asked Jake.

"Considering I know you about you and Jamal. No, not really," he growled loud enough for everyone to still hear.

Jamal's face dipped and a small gasp escaped. A gasp that sang of regret.

"Okay if you're about to turn and go full wolver on us, I'd like the option to change cars too," Celinde grunted as she faced Jake.

"I didn't sleep with him!" Kitty yelled.

"Kissing is enough, Kitty. You shouldn't be here!" Jake yelled.

"Is that how you all feel too?" She looked between Izzy, me, and Celinde.

"Sorry Kitty, but if all you can contribute is problems, maybe you should go home," Celinde answered.

Kitty climbed back out of the car as I started the ignition. She was angry and kicking the car as Jake ignored her and refused to look back.

"I'm sorry you had to witness that," he sighed with embarrassment.

"Oh, Jake! You don't need to apologize. I used to babysit you and I know you are a stand-up guy," Izzy hugged him.

"Kitty just never grew up," Jake sighed.

"We're only a few miles from the bunker, I think that might've been the agent who just sped past us," I announced trying desperately to change the conversation.

Hearing about Jake's personal life and having it made common knowledge among all of us wasn't the way we should be starting our new lives. He'd be open to embarrassment and shame from a handful of people who didn't even know him.

"I can see the realtor's car," Celinde smiled.

Thank goodness, that would release me from this for a while.

We pulled up and I leapt from the car eager to escape the disaster that had been unfolded.

"Hi! I'm Carrie," I smiled as I met the tall Italian man who held the keys and a think folder.

"Carrie! Doug, nice to finally meet you," he reached to shake my hand.

"Quite a drive, are you all doomsday preppers?" he joked.

"Not quite," I smiled as I brushed off his joke.

"Well, let's get started," he walked to the door, opened the folder, and keyed in a complex string of numbers and letters.

"There's instructions on how to change the code once you occupy the bunker," he noted.

Jax and Celinde crept up behind me so they could learn the finer details also. They quickly introduced themselves to Doug and then we carried on with the opening.

"It's going to need a good clean!" He sighed as he slid the door open.

"What was this place?" Jax asked.

"The information we got was that it was a laboratory base for a bunch of international scientists. Lots to learn in this empty part of the world," he smiled.

"Okay, down the middle is the mess and general areas, left and right are accommodations," he explained as he pointed down each hallway.

Tristan headed off first to explore the housing situation. We followed him as Doug pointed out lighting controls, heating, and all the other finer details. Each hall was color-coded to the folder and a Jax was intently listening to every word he said.

Mindy, Arthur, and Alexa found the first family quarters, it was huge, like a normal-sized house with all the comforts of home.

"The other housing wing is identical to this one, let's see the kitchen, shall we?" he asked.

"Yes!" gleamed Izzy.

Izzy was the picture of perfection, her home was immaculately clean, and she loved to cook, she had been eager to get stuck into an industrial-sized kitchen, Mindy was similar, although she seemed to focus more attention on Alexa. She was a mischievous child from what I could tell, but she brought a spark of innocence and energy to the group that was warmly welcomed. Austin's background as a teacher appealed to Mindy, she had discussed this in-depth with Alexa on the ride here, explaining that Austin would be tutoring her from now on and her grades had no excuse to slip now that she'd be working one on one. Austin of course had no idea.

The kitchen tour began with an oversized pantry and Christian and Kyle were already hauling goods into the storeroom while Izzy unpacked boxes of instant ramen, dozens upon dozens of eggs, and appliances such as bread makers and waffle irons.

"They aren't wasting any time," Doug chuckled.

Izzy puffed as she dropped a box of bacon into the fridge. Henry was hauling toilet paper in with Jamal and Otis had the mop buckets.

"Laundry?" I asked.

"Just down that hallway," he pointed to the left beside the four ovens.

"Five washers and three dryers, there's a storage room through that door," he pointed.

The rest of the tour came to an end quickly and Doug handed us the keys while Jax signed through a pile of paperwork.

"Thanks for your help," we said as both took turns to shake his hand.

"Okay, let's get the shady shit inside," Jax laughed as he and Christian hauled in boxes of thick chains, padlocks, and building tools.

"What is that?" I asked.

"Insurance," Christian sighed as Celinde came into his view.

"Christian suggested we have some backup. In the event we have a power failure on the wrong night. It's just precautionary, we intend to be away from here on those nights," Jax assured me.

"Away?" Celinde seemed squeamish at the thought.

"Yeah, we agreed we can't be our *natural* selves in here without destroying the place, we'll build some cabins and lockup who can't contain their urges, the rest can hunt animals freely," Jax explained.

"Well, it makes sense. It would keep this place clean," Celinde nodded.

"I will be locking myself up," Christian grasped her hands softly and held them to his chest.

"I'll help," she smiled.

"Arthur and Otis are already sourcing wood and materials to get started, they both don't trust themselves to be roaming,"

"Where's Ezra, Liam, and Austin?" I asked as I realized they had missed the tour.

"I saw them change and pounce away into the trees. Ezra wanted to check out the area and see if there's any humans close by," Jax explained.

"He changed?" Celinde asked.

"I trust him Cel, he's been at this a long time," I urged to silence her concern.

"You're going to have to get used to us bounding off into the forest babe," Christian stammered as he tested the waters of bab-er-y.

"I think what's important is that you two find a room," Jax cackled louder than I'd ever heard from him before.

Christian hung his head in shame and Celinde turned a shade of red almost brighter than my hair.

Tristan could be heard laughing from the mess hallway and Mindy and Izzy swooned as they latched onto the excitement of new uncharted love as if we were living in a romance novel.

"These halls are empty, and they echo," Jake smacked Jax on the back and chuckled loudly.

"Smut, please be smutty and let us revel in it," Mindy pleaded as she hugged Celinde and pointed to an empty room already furnished.

"Shall I wash the sheets?" Izzy pined as she clung to Mindy.

"Middle-aged women, all they do is housework, read absolute smut and withhold sex from their husbands," Arthur laughed as he brought in more power tools.

"You gotta admit Arthur, Christian has rock hard abs under that jacket, you have a phantom pregnancy," Mindy laughed.

"Mindy!" I laughed as I dropped my jaw and covered Tristan's ears.

"Do I get my own room? Tell me I get my own room?" Tristan begged and dropped to the ground.

"You can bunk with me bro," Kyle offered him his hand to pull him up.

"Oh, hell yeah! Can we bring chicks here?" he beamed.

"No, you can go to town for that business," Jax barked.

"Guess you're coming…" Tristan teased.

"Only for the beers," Jax smiled.

"Guess that's you too," Mindy poked Arthur in the belly.

"Ugh, you're a witch," he laughed as he grabbed her and kissed her softly.

"Aww," Celinde cooed.

"Rock hard abs over here…" Christian pointed to himself while she glared at him.

"Okay let's go clean that room," she grabbed his hand and they raced off.

"Izzy's already in there fluffing pillows and changing the linen," I laughed.

"Okay, well we have an abundance of Costco pizzas, that'll be dinner," Mindy announced.

I followed her to the kitchen and turned on the ovens while she pulled out 8 pizzas and froze the remainder.

"How many of those do we have?" I asked.

"Another twenty," she counted.

"And apparently five boxes of candy bars," she held up mixed boxes of Reece's and other sugary treats.

"Those are mine!" Tristan admitted as he walked into the kitchen following his nose.

"Hungry?" I asked.

"Famished," he nodded.

"Don't worry these don't take long, it'll be dark soon, are the others still outside?" Mindy asked.

"Jax and Arthur went for a run to find them all," he answered.

"I see...let's not tell Celinde that. She's been edgy," I held out my pinkie for him to promise.

"She's coming around," Tristan assured me.

"Well, just to be safe," I winced.

Ezra walked into the kitchen first and he inhaled the smell of pizza animatedly. Liam was behind him, and Alexa was following Austin, interrogating him about schooling.

"Alexa, leave Austin to eat his dinner," Mindy insisted.

"I'd be happy to help Mindy, I have nothing better to do," he smiled.

"I'd appreciate that so much," Mindy smiled back as she passed him a slice of cheese pizza.

"So, tomorrow you can come out and build with us. First lesson, woodwork," Austin went to give her knuckles.

"No!" she exclaimed with disappointment and smirked as she refused the knuckles.

"I'm a girl, I don't build!" she said smugly.

"Ahhh, yeah. She's feisty, strong-minded," Mindy sighed.

"Like her feisty mother," Arthur announced as he walked into the kitchen covered in dirt.

"Where the hell have you been?" Mindy scowled.

"In the forest marking out plots for the cabins. There's a clearing a mile from here, it's flat and we've posted markers," he explained.

I pulled out the last of the pizzas from the ovens and laid them on the bench for everyone to help themselves.

V.J.Garland

Chapter Twelve

Christian

I picked up Celinde and carried her out our door and into the hallway to go and eat dinner with the others.

Jax closed the main door to the bunker. Everyone set about getting comfortable in their rooms and finding things they wanted from the other spare rooms.

Izzy had everyone's linens washed and dried in record timing and called everyone in individually to collect their clean sheets.

"You're a powerhouse Izzy!" I hugged her when she called for me.

"Will I need to call for Ezra?" she at Carrie

"Umm," She sighed.

Ezra entered the room and like a true gentleman he placed out his hands for his linens.

"Well, he's a true gentleman," Izzy smiled.

"That he is, I don't have that restraint," I laughed.

"How are things with Celinde?" Izzy asked.

"Better! A lot better," I smiled.

It was comforting to talk to someone new about it and Izzy and Mindy seemed to be in our corner cheering us on. Now Carrie was warming up to Ezra and Kyle was in a world of torment, I was glad he wasn't like the rest of us. He put on a brave face, but I could smell his jealousy when Ezra so much as glanced at her. He played friendly, but he wasn't looking to make a new friend. I liked Kyle, but this brought out an ugly in him that I could not have imagined before.

"She'll be okay. Kyle's human, what can he really do?" Izzy assured me.

"I've been a firefighter for ten years. Humans can be far worse than werewolves," I pressed my lips together tightly and sighed as we shared a worried look between us.

"Henry and I will look out for him," Izzy nodded.

"I'm glad we found you guys," I hugged her and walked away to my room with the clean sheets.

Celinde was in the doorway to our room with a cheesy grin on her face and two glasses of champagne. She passed one to me and I drank it quickly. I was eager to escape the others and reset in solitude.

"I think I could call this home," Celinde smiled as she brushed her dark blonde hair in the mirror.

"For how long?" I doubted.

"What do you mean?" She asked.

"This isn't permanent, it can't be. We can't live out the next fifty or sixty years in a bunker. It's just a means to an end," I sighed.

"Once everyone finds self-control, we'll all leave this place, Christian," she knelt before me and held my hands.

"What if that never happens?" I gushed.

"Then we stay, for as long as we need," She pressed.

"Why the doubt?" She sighed.

"Ezra has been a wolf for ten years…" I confessed.

"And he has the most control, I saw him transition before he ran into the forest. It was so fluid and controlled," She squeezed my hand with hope and for a second, I saw the Celinde I had met at the fire station. The innocent one who smiled from ear to ear with wavy hair framing her face, kind eyes, and soft lips.

"He hasn't aged Celinde, I opened his wallet at dinner. He was born in '75. He still looks thirty," I felt puzzled, joyful, and lost all in one pulse.

"He's older than Arthur?" she now had that same puzzled look I felt in my expression.

"Maybe we just don't age now?" I pondered.

"Ask him about it?" she suggested.

"Tomorrow," I agreed.

"For now, let's go for a walk?" I asked.

"A walk? It's freezing!" She shuddered.

"Chuck this on, it'll keep you warm," I threw her my turnout coat I'd taken from the truck before we ditched it.

"Okay, let's go," She smiled.

The door to the bunker was already cracked open slightly.

"I swear Jax closed that..." Celinde stammered.

"He did," I muttered.

I approached the door first and peeled it open some. Jake, Ezra, Liam, and Tristan were outside already with concerned looks on their faces. Jake was panting, his face smeared with dirt and blood as scratches from branches slowly healed before our eyes.

"Is everything okay?" Celinde asked.

"Kitty's out there, Kyle's trying to talk her down, but she's inconsolable. She was under the impression we would turn back for her," Jake groaned.

"Did she do that to you?" I asked.

"I let her take a few swings, but she swung a branch at me and sent me down that ravine we passed on the way in," Jake replied.

"But Kyle?" I asked.

"He's human. I hoped she'd listen to him," he explained.

Celinde walked off to look for them and I stayed back with Jake and the others making sure the shouting didn't wake the others who were already asleep.

It was hard to make out words between Kitty's wailing, Kyle just sounded irritated and Celinde was trying her best to calm Kitty as she walked her toward us.

Jake walked back into the bunker. It was obvious he cared for her safety, but she was no longer welcome.

"Let's clean you up, and tomorrow we'll take you into town and call your family," Celinde mumbled as she moved Kitty past us all quickly.

"She's a liability…" Jake sighed.

"Nobody would believe her, and she'd never remember the way back here, she might disappear," Tristan added jokingly.

"Is that what happens to humans around you *people?*" Kyle snapped.

"You'll just kill anyone who gets in your way?" he tried to get in Ezra's face as he pushed Tristan in a fit of rage.

"Kyle!" I growled.

"You're the worst offender Christian! You were hell-bent on leaving us behind, you should have!" he yelled.

"I had no say in any of this. Jax is running this circus. If you have a problem, take it up with him!" I yelled.

Jax emerged from the door rubbing his tired eyes.

"What the fuck is all the yelling about?" Jax was pissed, he hardly ever swore.

"Kyle needs to join the pack and let off some steam," Ezra gripped him by the shirt and threw him to Jax's feet.

"Do you want to be one of us?" Jax asked.

"Do I have a choice? I'm stuck here! It's bound to happen eventually!" he yelled.

"Be careful Kyle, this is dangerous territory," Ezra warned.

"One way to find out!" He punched Jax in the face.

Jax spat blood onto the dirt and wiped his chin with his wrist.

"Let it out, Kyle," Jax said calmly.

Jax wasn't ready to hit his best friend, but he took every hit and never dropped to the ground. Hit after hit, kick after kick, Kyle threw Jax around like a ragdoll and he allowed it.

"Hit me back, Jax!" Kyle roared.

"If I hit you, I won't stop," Jax pressed his foot into his shoulder and held him down in the snow. His shirt was torn open, blood from his face dripping down his chest as he panted loudly.

Tristan bowed his head sadly and moved to my side and turned away from the violence, Ezra was covering his ears and pulling at his long hair, Liam and Jake had retreated in front of the door to stop a sneaky Alexa from coming outside to witness further conflict.

"But you're their leader now… and if I kill you, I kill them too," Kyle smiled, his eyes dark as he licked a droplet of Jax's blood from his lip.

He reached for a sharp thick branch and lunged to plunge it into Jax's chest, but Jax was faster. In a blink, Jax's claws were deep in his chest, and screams echoed over the mountains and throughout the valley.

"Oh fuck!" Tristan yelled as blood sprayed over us.

"Jax!" I yelled.

Kyle's chest was slashed open so deep and so wide I could see his heart slowing.

"Fuck!" Jax cried as he examined the blood splattered on his hands.

"Carrie!" Jake yelled as he rushed inside.

"Celinde!" Liam screamed.

Jax's hands morphed back, and he dropped to his side.

"I'm so sorry," he cried.

Carrie and Celinde rushed out with first aid bags, but nothing prepared them for what they saw, he was split down from the bone.

"He could still turn?" Carrie cried as she looked to Ezra for guidance.

"Not everyone turns Carrie," he sighed as he held Kyle's hand.

Everyone stood around as we waited and listened for signs of an awakening, but there was nothing, just the sound of the wind, teardrops as they hit our cheeks, veins emptying themselves into the road and, the warmth of Kyle's blood dissipating into the snow.

"Inside, Alexa," Tristan grabbed her hand and walked her back to her room where I heard the conversation unfold.

Tristan was in tears; he had truly adopted us all as family and once again he'd lost someone.

"What happened to Kyle?" Alexa questioned.

Tristan took a deep breath, swallowed his sadness, and hugged her as he took on the big brother role so naturally and explained the conflict in a more juvenile language.

"He's not waking up!" Jax growled.

"He didn't want this! He isn't going to turn, it was too much for him," I grabbed Jax and tried to calm him.

"I killed him," he was shaken and staring into nothing.

"Bury the body…" Jax ordered, his eyes darkened, as he sprung off into the woods.

"Should we go after him?" Jake asked.

"No, he needs to be alone," Carrie answered.

"Izzy, can we have some sheets to wrap the body in please?" Celinde asked through tears as Izzy patted her hair gently.

"I'll grab them," Mindy nodded as she rubbed her tired and tormented eyes.

Austin and Arthur came out with shovels, they'd heard it all from inside, the others choosing not to witness the darkness of this night.

"Celinde, give Kitty my car, tell her never to come back here!" Jake pressed the keys into her hand as he retreated inside.

"Can you hear that?" Carrie asked as she looked around.

"Sounds like thunder," I replied.

"It's not…" Ezra raced to the edge of the road and looked out into the clearing. Jax was uprooting the forestry in the designated areas for cabins.

"If you're not helping bury Kyle, back to your rooms," I ordered. I knew anyone out wandering was going to get themselves in Jax's way, and we couldn't afford that right now.

Tristan came out to help me, Carrie, and Ezra with the body. It wasn't anything special. A deep hole in a large mound half a mile from the bunker, another unmarked grave in the middle of nowhere.

Chapter Thirteen

Carrie

It took days for Jax to speak to any of us, he never came inside. He just built, he built log cabin after log cabin until there were ten. Well-spaced apart, complete with mini-kitchens and bathrooms and a lot of hardware and chains of the torturous kind.

Once he was done, he took us all for a tour of the new lodgings.

"This is where you'll stay when you're out of control, this is where I'll be until I can be controlled..." he sighed.

As we walked away from the last log cabin farthest from the bunker, we caught a smell. The smell of death and decomposing bodies, there was a whole herd of moose piled to the side of Jax's cabin.

"Oh gross," Celinde covered her mouth as she almost gagged from the smell.

"So, we're captives now?" I asked Christian.

"Not as long as you stay within the Precinct," Jax yelled.

A precinct, google translates that to *'an area in a town designated for specific or restricted use, especially one which is closed to traffic'.*

We were trapped here... In Jax's personal hell, in his Precinct.

V.J.Garland

V.J.Garland